W9-CMC-251

BROKEN SONG

BROKEN SONG

KATHRYN LASKY

VIKING

VIKING
Published by Penguin Group
Penguin Young Readers Group, 345 Hudson Street, New York, New York 10014, U.S.A.
Penguin Group (Canada), 10 Alcorn Avenue, Toronto, Ontario, Canada M4V 3B2
(a division of Pearson Penguin Canada Inc.)
Penguin Books Ltd, 80 Strand, London WC2R 0RL, England
Penguin Ireland, 25 St Stephen's Green, Dublin 2, Ireland
(a division of Penguin Books Ltd)
Penguin Group (Australia), 250 Camberwell Road, Camberwell, Victoria 3124, Australia
(a division of Pearson Australia Group Pty Ltd)
Penguin Books India Pvt Ltd, 11 Community Centre, Panchsheel Park,
New Delhi - 110 017, India
Penguin Group (NZ), Cnr Airborne and Rosedale Roads, Albany, Auckland,
New Zealand (a division of Pearson New Zealand Ltd)
Penguin Books (South Africa) (Pty) Ltd, 24 Sturdee Avenue, Rosebank, Johannesburg 2196, South Africa
Penguin Books Ltd, Registered Offices: 80 Strand, London WC2R 0RL, England

Published in the U.S.A. by Viking, a division of Penguin Young Readers Group, 2005

1 3 5 7 9 10 8 6 4 2

LIBRARY OF CONGRESS CATALOGING-IN-PUBLICATION DATA
Lasky, Kathryn.
Broken song / by Kathryn Lasky.
p. cm.
Summary: In 1897, fifteen-year-old Reuven Bloom, a Russian Jew, must set aside his dreams of playing the violin in order to save himself and his baby sister after the rest of their family is murdered.
ISBN 0-670-05931-5 (hardcover)
1. Jews—Russia—History—19th century—Juvenile fiction. [1. Jews—Russia—History—19th century—Fiction. 2. Violin—Fiction. 3. Brothers and sisters—Fiction. 4. Persecution—Fiction. 5. Russia—History—Nicholas II, 1894–1917—Fiction.] I. Title.
PZ7.L3274Br 2005
[Fic]—dc22
2004017741

Printed in U.S.A. Set in Bembo Book design by Sam Kim

For my grandparents,
who endured these times.
—K. L.

Part I

RUSSIA

1897

ONE

"TOO MUCH! Too much vibrato!" Herschel the violin teacher muttered. "You don't like too much flour in the sauce. It disguises the taste. Vibrato works the same way. Too much disguises the real music. Why would you do such a thing to Bach?"

Because, thought Reuven to himself, *I am not thinking of Bach. I am thinking of your father's beard.* Reb Itchel sat at a table by a small window, bent over his prayer books. The sun streamed through the window and turned the old man's beard even whiter. It curled off his chin like wisps of smoke. Reuven became hypnotized by it as he played his violin. The music seemed to flow through him directly to the little beard. And the funny part was that the rebbe was deaf—stone deaf. He bent and rocked to his own music, lost in the ancient Hebrew prayers. He existed in some misty place filled with the voices of the old rabbis.

The little beard jerked up. Reb Itchel suddenly emerged from the mists. He muttered in Yiddish to his son Herschel.

"Yes, yes, Papa, I know. It's the first day of Passover. I must dismiss Reuven early today."

As Reuven put down his bow and the music stopped, he blinked. The beard was just a beard again.

"So," Herschel said. "I shall see you tomorrow right after school, Reuven. No practice time tonight because of seder. We shall continue with the Bach and take a little time, if you can, to look at the Brahms Concerto in D major."

Reuven tucked his violin case under his arm, made his way out of the muddy front yard of his violin teacher's cottage, and turned down the road. He had to pick his way carefully. The world had turned to mud. Spring had finally come. Reuven did not mind the mud. He felt it was a fair trade for the stain of green that was finally coming back to the trees, the little white and blue flowers that popped from the earth with blossoms no bigger than his baby sister's fingernails. While he thought of all this, the notes from the Bach concerto swirled through his head and the callused fingers of his right hand, his bow hand, unconsciously plucked at invisible strings.

It seemed, however, that woven between the sucking noises of the mud under his boots, the fragrance of new green hovering in the air, and the music in his head, there was something else that he must think about, something else pressing on his brain, something he did not want to acknowledge. A bleakness at the edge of his mind. Prakova! The single word exploded in his head. It was another shtetl, a small village in the Pale, the only region in Russia where Jews were allowed to settle. Last year on Passover, the entire village of Prakova had been burned, every living thing killed. There was not even a dog left. And the Cossacks had been so clever. They had first ridden through some weeks before and kidnapped every able-bodied young man and boy, and then they had left the rest of the job to the peasants who had been incited to hate Jews. It was the worst pogrom in recent memory.

It was impossible to anticipate any holiday with joy, only fear, since Prakova. And it seemed that the tsar and the Cossacks and the peasants took special delight now in disrupting the holiest of days for the Jews in the Pale. How could he, Reuven Bloom, have forgotten this and instead been almost skipping through the mud to the allegro of the Bach concerto? What a fool he was!

And then as if to remind him of his foolishness, a fierce squawk came from a dreary little cottage set on spindly pilings.

"Reuven Bloom, you no-good dreamer!" It was Reb Mendel, the teacher in the religious school for very young boys. How happy Reuven was to be fifteen now and no longer under Reb Mendel's rule. Reb Mendel and his family lived in a house that reminded Reuven of a scrawny chicken, and the teacher himself, with his puckered yellow flesh, seemed more chicken than human. How often Reuven had dreamed of throwing him in a pot. And, being no fool, Reuven imagined that Reb Mendel had dreamed similar dreams for him. Reuven had been his least favorite student.

"So, still fiddling? Still trying to make music rather than listen to the holy music of the Talmud?"

Whenever Reuven saw or had to speak to Reb Mendel, he had an instinctive reaction to cover his ears. Twisting young scholars' ears had been the rebbe's favorite form of punishment. He would twist and pinch boys' ears so hard that they would turn white in some places from having the blood circulation cut off. Reuven could still hear the terrible black buzzy sound that would roar first in his ears and then spread into his skull when Reb Mendel did this.

"So, I understand your friend Muttle is making great progress." Reb Mendel paused and plucked at the folds of waxy skin that drooped from his neck like the wattle of an old rooster.

There was another squawk from the mean little house. It was the teacher's wife yelling, and then some dirty children scampered out ahead of her.

"Oh Reuven, Reuven play music for us!" they called. Reuven looked down at the children. *They need something beautiful*, he thought, *living in this place with their dreary parents.*

He opened his violin case. Reb Mendel groaned, but the children squealed with delight. Reuven drew his bow across the strings. The first notes came soft as the birds on the warm spring drafts. The children stilled. Then quick silvery music laced the air. Reuven looked down at the smudged little faces. One child's eye was red and nearly swollen shut. But they grew quiet and looked up, their small mouths parted as if to receive the music. *How grim to be a child of Reb Mendel*, thought Reuven. *How completely grim!*

When he had finished playing, the teacher's wife came over to him.

"So you're really growing up, Reuven Bloom. A nice handsome lad. But why can't you be like your good friend Muttle? What woman is going to want a man who never studies? Look at my husband here. When he is not teaching little fools like you who grow up to fiddle, he studies all day. Was there anyone ever more fit for the afterlife than my husband?"

Fit for the afterlife? Yes, Reuven wanted to say, *if heaven is a chicken coop.*

"Ahh," sighed Reb Mendel. "Who's to know, my dear? Why would a fellow like Muttle ever want to be with this piece of trouble?" It was unbelievable. They were insulting him to his face after he had played music for their children. Well, let them insult his back, at least. He began to walk away.

"Why? Tell me this!" Reb Mendel lifted his hands dramatically toward the sky, as if asking God for an answer. Reuven heard one of the children giggle. He turned around. Several of the little ones were trailing after him.

"Why, Reb Mendel?" Reuven shouted. "I'll tell you why Muttle likes me; because I make music!" And he ran down the muddy road toward the village. If he hurried, he might catch Muttle.

~ TWO ~

"MUTTLE!" REUVEN called as he caught sight of the long tails of a coat billowing in the breeze. Reuven ran down Krochner Street and saw Muttle disappear through the door of the herring shop. He ran in after him, clapping his friend on the back.

"I looked for you at the study house," Reuven said. "Where were you?"

"I left early because I had to pick up this herring for my mother."

"Keep your hands out of there!" Fruma the herring woman yelled at a small boy. "No nose pickers in my herring barrels." She reached in and swished her hands through the briny water.

"Here, Muttle, your mother likes these." She held up a long fillet of herring. The silver and dark strips of the skin glistened. "Fit for a scholar." She sighed and winked.

Reuven saw that Muttle was blushing. It was impossible, with his fair skin, to hide it, and now his whole face was the color of his pale red hair. Reuven wondered what kind of herring was fit for a violinist.

"And here's a little extra for you to have now," Fruma said. She wrapped the fillets in two pieces of paper.

"Come on," said Muttle. "Let's go eat this in peace before we have to be home. I'm starved."

There was a great bustle in all the streets of Berischeva as people raced the setting sun to prepare for the first seder dinner of Passover. There were wonderful smells coming through all the windows and doors of the hunched little buildings and squat cottages—chickens roasting and vegetables and fruits stewing with sprinklings of cinnamon. Reuven wondered why cinnamon was not used as much at other times of the year. He and Muttle passed a doorway where a girl their age and her younger sister wept horseradish tears as they grated the strong white root into a bowl for the seder table.

Finally they came to a path that led to the river, and on the banks they settled down with their herring.

"So is it true what Reb Mendel and others say, that you have memorized most of the commentaries in the Talmud?" Reuven asked.

Muttle made a short harsh sound halfway between a snort and a laugh. "More like half," he answered, and took another bite.

Reuven blew a long low whistle. "Still, incredible! How do you do it? You'll be like a living book. You'll have the memory, the tradition for everyone right up here." Reuven tapped his head.

Muttle laughed again. "Even for you!"

That was what was good about Muttle. He could joke about his friend's lack of knowledge, and yet Reuven never felt as if he were being mocked.

"I should study harder, I know." Reuven sighed.

"Why?" Muttle asked, genuinely shocked. His pale brow puckered. "You think we need two living books walking around Russia? Are you crazy?"

"But, Muttle, every year it gets worse for Jews. New laws, new pogroms. They run us off the land, they kill us. If anyone is left, who will know the tradition?"

"Who will be left to play music? You carry the music, Reuven. I carry the words," Muttle said. Then he picked up a flat stone and skipped it across the water.

As they walked home, Reuven thought about the unlikeliness of their friendship. Maybe that was what made it so valuable. No one could ever say that Muttle and Reuven were as alike as two peas in a pod. Muttle was pale, painfully thin, short, and frail, like a red leaf ready to blow away. Reuven was husky and dark, with intense blue eyes that blazed out from under a thatch of unruly black hair.

They had been friends, best friends, since they first met in religious school when they were four years old. Muttle was so quick he learned the entire Hebrew alphabet in a few days. But Reuven could play music before he could read it. Then when Herschel Itchel came to town when Reuven was just six, he learned to read music as quickly as Muttle had learned to read Hebrew.

They walked partway to their homes together in silence. Good friends, really good friends, didn't need to talk all the time. They each seemed to sense what the other was thinking. The bleakness now seemed to be hovering at the edge of both of their minds. How wrong it seemed to be thinking of Prakova when they were about to begin to celebrate Passover—the Jews' deliverance from slavery! Pharaohs, tsars—would they never just disappear and leave the Jews alone?

THREE

THE COTTAGE on Petrova Street where Reuven lived seemed to lurch to one side. One could imagine it to be lame, like an old man or woman who favored one leg because of an arthritic hip joint. The thatched roof sagged over the front doorway. It reminded Reuven of one long bushy eyebrow. There was a girl in the marketplace who sold candles—she had eyebrows like that. They grew together into one long brow. His mother and older sister, Shriprinka, had endless conversations about this girl and her eyebrow. *It's such an easy thing to fix, and she's in the candle business. All she needs to do is melt some candle wax and drip it between her eyes. Two seconds and that hair would be gone—just peel off the wax. How will she ever get a husband? All because of one lousy eyebrow . . .*

Reuven himself wondered if he could ever love a girl with one eyebrow. It seemed like such a silly thing to make a fuss about, but nonetheless he wondered.

"Ahk, ahk, ahk . . ." The fat little baby girl turned around and squealed with delight as Reuven came into the house. She banged harder on a pot with a wooden spoon. Except for Rachel banging on the pot, everything was in quiet order. The seder table was set with a gleaming white cloth that fell like thick cream over the surface. The wineglasses were filled. Reuven's father, Aaron Bloom, stood ready while his sister, Shriprinka, brought the bowls for hand washing to the table. Reuven's mother, Bathshepa, was about to light the candles.

"Where's Uncle Chizor?" Reuven asked, and scooped up his baby sister.

"Any minute," his father said, looking at his watch. "He's just back from Poland."

"Aah, the baron." Shriprinka sighed. Reuven knew what she was thinking. How she would have loved to see the estate near Bryznck where their uncle went three times a year to tailor clothes for the wealthy Baron Radzinsky. He stayed in the palatial manor house on the baron's estate. The baron was not a Jew-hater like so many of the Russian and Polish nobility. He loved Chizor and showered him with presents. Chizor ordered the most luxurious fabrics for the baron. He made him everything from evening clothes and fur-trimmed capes to elegant brocaded smoking jackets. The fabrics were often French, sometimes Chinese, and other times Scottish wools. Reuven loved his uncle's tales of the baron. They had all sat enthralled the first time Uncle Chizor described the long drive leading into the estate, which was lined with white oak trees. Two huge marble lions flanked either side of the entrance of the stone and timber mansion. And then there were the gardens. There was one where only white flowers grew. Another was just for roses. There were vineyards and orchards and an outdoor and an indoor court for playing a game called tennis.

"Reuven," said his mother. "Please go get another bottle of wine from the potato hole." Reuven put down his baby sister and walked to a corner by the window. He pulled a square-cut plank from the floor and bent down to reach for the bottle of wine. Almost every cottage had a potato hole for root vegetables, but the Bloom family's was unusually large. They kept bottles of wine, bags of sugar, and sacks of grain there. It was so big that Reuven's mother constantly fussed about putting the plank back for fear that Rachel would fall in. Rachel was right by Reuven's knees now as he bent down into the deep darkness of the hole.

"Back, Rachel, back. You don't want to fall in here and crack your head."

Shriprinka came and grabbed Rachel by the sashes on her dress. "You'll get all dirty in there, Rachel," she said. "There are spiders and dirt and cobwebs. It's no place for you in your pretty seder dress."

Just as Reuven came up from the hole with the extra bottle of wine, there was the sound of footsteps outside. The door opened, and a large man with a jet-black beard flecked with silver swirled in.

"Shalom, shalom aleichem!" he cried merrily. "I bring you gifts from the baron."

"Ahk, ahk, ahk." Rachel was tugging on the tails of his gabardine.

"Oh, you want something too. If I pick you up, no

eyebrow pulling." He shook his finger at Rachel. Uncle Chizor had thick black eyebrows, and each one had a tuft of white at the inside corner, which Rachel's chubby hands always went for. "Well, this is really a gift for all of us, although it will be up to Reuven to 'deliver it' so to speak."

"What are you talking about, Uncle?" Reuven asked.

From a deep inside pocket, Chizor Bloom withdrew several sheaves of paper with small dark marks. "Music—sheet music—the Czech fellow."

"Dvořák!" Reuven exclaimed. "Antonín Dvořák?"

"That's the one."

"You brought me music of Antonín Dvořák?" Reuven could hardly believe it. Sheet music and scores were hard enough to come by in the Pale, but music of Dvořák was especially rare. And yet every music student and music lover in Europe had heard of this great composer who had begun as a violinist. "Oh, Uncle," Reuven said in awe. "The baron gave it to you just like that?"

Chizor snapped his fingers. "Like that," he said. Was it such a surprise really? The baron had already found the Ceruti violin that Reuven played. Ceruti violins, made in Cremona, were among the finest in the world. They were also extremely expensive.

"Ready?" asked Bathshepa. Reuven set aside the sheet music and picked up Rachel again. She gurgled and pulled at his hair as Bathshepa struck the match. The candlesticks were real silver. They were the most valuable things that the Bloom family owned. The candles glowed a pale yellow just like the water flowers that

Reuven had seen once in a remote creek. From one tiny window the last ray of the day's sun flared like a smear of pale blood on the pane.

Then the seder began.

This was Reuven's fifteenth Passover, and each time he found it just as wonderful as the last. This time even more so, perhaps because it was baby Rachel's first seder. Having a baby at a seder was perfect, because babies made everything so imperfect. She got carried away with the hand washing and splashed all the water out of the bowl. She tried to stick the parsley up her nose, then thought that was so funny she stuck some in her ear. How would Rachel know that the parsley at the seder table symbolized hope and spring? It was fun to tickle your nose with it.

They all laughed at Rachel, and the more they laughed, the wilder she got. After the seder, Reuven got out his violin and played. He tried the Dvořák. It was as if the composer's hands lay lightly on his own. The piece was a slow romantic one. It was sheer intuition that led Reuven to play the opening measures with great calmness. Even Rachel stopped her fidgeting and seemed captivated by the melody.

That night as he went to bed, Reuven thought how especially wonderful this seder had been. He was not tired, and he could not fall asleep. Often on warm spring or summer nights, Reuven went up onto the roof of the little house to watch the stars. Tonight as he came out on the roof, he was thinking of Rachel. He looked up at the sky and saw the stars swirling in the deep black. *The stars are so old*, he thought, *and she is so young*. She has been on this earth for only eleven months. Her first seder.

Rachel had been born blue . . . blue as the sky, blue as a violet. But once one has seen a baby born blue, it is hard to think of violets and sky. Blue is wrong. That is all Reuven thought at the time. He was standing in the shadows of the cottage when she was born, but he saw. The midwife slapped her. She sucked on Rachel's tiny mouth, and finally Reuven was sent to fetch a bucket of freezing cold water. The ice on the river had just broken up. He had never run so fast. Luckily the river was near. They plunged her in the bucket. There was a sound that was like a bubble bursting, and then not a little whimper, but a yowl. A big angry yowl. Even the midwife was surprised. She said most babies born blue, if they live, don't yowl, they whimper. But it was clearly a mistake that Rachel had been born blue. It was almost as if she were saying blue *is* for violets, blue *is* for birds, blue *is not* for me. She was mad, very mad. How could this mistake have been made? An outrage! She wailed.

In Reuven's mind, Rachel had been trying to prove how alive she was ever since. And that is what made this Passover special. This fat baby tyrant, who stuffed parsley up her nose and blew bubbles into her tiny cup of wine, was a miracle by virtue of her very existence. It was Rachel who sang all the seder songs the loudest. "Blah gah gah gah." It all made sense to her because after you've been born dead, there is no real logic. As they were singing the last song, Rachel scrambled down onto the floor. She stood with no hands holding on to anything, swaying like a tipsy man from a tavern. Everyone kept singing, but their eyes were fastened on the baby. Then she took a step, a very first step. And everyone gasped and stopped singing.

"She is walking to Jerusalem!" Aaron Bloom whispered, as if he thought the breath of his words might topple her.

Reuven was thinking of all this when Shriprinka climbed up beside him on the roof.

"Couldn't sleep?" he asked.

"The cricket is back."

"It is!"

"Yes, it always takes some getting used to for me," Shriprinka said, and laughed softly.

"I like him."

"I know. You hear music in everything."

"Where do you think he goes in winter?"

"The *Goldeneh Medina,* the Golden Country, America, where else?" She laughed.

"Maybe Chicago."

"Chi—what?" His sister's gray eyes opened like huge pale stars in the night. He had known this would impress her.

"Chicago. It's a big city in America. I've heard about it."

"You mean there's more than New York?"

"Oh yes, there's San Francisco and Denver and Atlanta and Philadelphia and Boston. . . ." The names rolled off his lips into the night, and Shriprinka stared at her brother in awe, as if he were playing the most beautiful violin piece.

"How do you know all this, Reuven? Wait . . ." She held up her hand. "Don't tell me. You go to the storybook man."

Reuven smiled and nodded. "But don't tell Mama and Papa."

"But Reuven, it's expensive. Isn't it?"

"No, he rents you two for a kopek. I found out about places like Denver through the cowboy stories."

"Cowboy stories?"

"Yes, stories about tough guys who ride horses and round up cattle out in the western part of America."

"Two books for a kopek, that's pretty good," Shriprinka said.

"You want me to rent you some?"

Shriprinka hunched her shoulders and giggled. "I don't know, Reuven."

"They've got romances for girls."

"What do I care about romances?"

"You don't?" Reuven didn't know that much about girls.

"No. I think I'd rather read stories about other places than here—about, you know, Chicago, Denver, San Francisco. And Phila . . ."

"Delphia."

"Yes. That's it. What do I care for romances? Romance is a waste of time."

"It is?" Reuven was surprised.

"You know that. Mama and Papa will go to the

matchmaker for me when the time comes, and what will romance have to do with it?"

Now all Reuven could think about was the girl in the marketplace with one eyebrow. What if a matchmaker thought the best match she could make for that girl was a boy who never studied Talmud and instead wasted his time on rented storybooks and the violin? Reuven sighed deeply and tipped his head up. The stars whirled in the sky.

Then it was as if Shriprinka could read his mind. She patted his hand.

"Don't worry, Reuven. You're safe from the matchmakers. They think you're a lazy dreamer. But somewhere out there is a girl who loves music. She will quiver when you play, and she won't care at all if you know Talmud or not."

He heard the cricket that night as he lay drifting off to sleep. He heard it shaping sounds with its legs. Was it the same cricket he and Shriprinka had heard last year, or was it the great-great-great-great-grandchild of the cricket he heard in this cottage when they had first moved here? That had been over ten years ago, after they had been forced from the village where he was born, the village he could hardly remember. But it had not been in the Pale. Maybe the cricket had come with them. Or was it a native, a Pale cricket? No matter, he liked its song. Someday he might write a concerto or even a symphony and it would have all the sounds of the land—the music of the cricket, the rush of the river, the stillness of the creek where the nameless yellow water flowers grew, and yes, the yowl of Rachel. He yawned and fell fast asleep.

FOUR

HIS LESSON had gone well. Once more he was passing by the spindly-legged chicken house of Reb Mendel. On the lapel of his gabardine coat he slid his first finger up an imaginary violin string, thinking how Herschel had said the beginning of the Bach should be played. Simply, without effort, but with restraint. "Restraint." Herschel had whispered the word. And then Reuven's thoughts were shattered.

"Did you hear me, you idiot boy? You no-good piece of ignorance! May a darkness be yours! Why not you? Those catchers—they got no sense. We will put you on the list next time—you piece of swine dropping!"

It was Reb Mendel, his eyes bulging out of his narrow head. He hopped first on one foot then the other. Flecks of spittle flew from his thin purple lips. He was screaming curses.

"What? What are you saying?" Reuven thought he heard Muttle's name. "What? What about Muttle?"

"They took him! You fool. The catchers came and grabbed him for the tsar's army."

"What? This is impossible."

"Yes. That is what I said. I said, how can they take the pride of our village? Our most gifted scholar. Why not take you? You could fiddle to the Cossacks. Yes, like

Nero . . ." The thin purple lips pulled back in a horrid grin, revealing yellow teeth that came to sharp points. "Yes, you could fiddle as they burn Jewish villages across Russia. That would suit you fine."

Reuven turned his back on the man's rantings and began running as fast as he could, as fast as the night when Rachel was born. All he could think of was that there must be some mistake. Why ever would they take Muttle? Muttle, who hardly weighed more than a sack of grain. How can a living book make a soldier?

As Reuven ran through the village, he noticed knots of people standing on the corners and gathered in doorways. There was an eerie quiet that seemed to have descended over everything. And was it his imagination, or did some of these people slide their eyes sideways and look at him, stealing a glance as he flew by? Were they wondering, *Why not Reuven? Why Muttle our scholar, God's blessing to this shtetl? Take the fiddler.*

"Is it true?" he gasped as he burst through the door. But he knew it was. Why else would his father be home from work? Why would Shriprinka be so deathly white and still on a stool in the corner? Why would his mother be clutching Rachel and trembling so hard? It was as if his mother had suddenly become an old lady. Her eyes seemed sunken and faded with that mixture of fear and confusion he had sometimes seen in old folks' eyes. Even Rachel seemed to know something was terribly wrong. She jammed her thumb into her mouth and looked as solemn as Reuven had ever seen her.

Reuven dropped to his knees by his mother's chair.

"I am here, Mama. I am here. Don't worry. They

don't want a fiddler." But she was not listening. A stream of colorless words in a near monotone came from her mouth in a strange mechanical voice.

"They came and they snatched him and Isaac the orphan right from the study house, him and Isaac. And two of the rebbes jumped up and said, 'No, not him' and they meant Muttle. They didn't bother to say, 'No, not Isaac.' Can you believe it, and they call themselves holy men?" There was no anger in her voice, but she continued reciting, as if she were trying to accustom herself to this tale of horror. "And then, you know, they did the usual. They went for the poor ones—the rag man's son Koppel, Shlomo the cobbler's boy, and then of course, any other orphans." His mother's voice dwindled off into the shadows that seemed to cling in the corners of the cottage.

That night when Reuven went to bed, he asked into the darkness, "Why?" But there was only the sound of the cricket.

FIVE

IN THE sleepy moments of the first morning that Reuven awakened after Muttle's kidnapping, he felt a terrible heaviness within him, and also a darkness. It was as if the shadows of the night had somehow crept into his body. It did not matter that it was daylight, that the sun shone with the bright ferocity of early spring. He was confused in those first minutes. He vaguely knew that something was terribly wrong—wrong with him? Wrong with the world? And yet he could not quite remember why he was feeling this deep sadness. Then it slid over him, just like the spots of sun on his blanket. His mind fully wakened to the reality. His best friend was gone.

That was the first morning. Now he had not grown accustomed to it, but he was no longer confused. It was the first thing he thought about every morning and the last thing at night, and then a thousand times during the day.

Seven weeks it had now been; almost fifty days had passed. Nothing had been normal, and yet everyone had to pretend it was. That was perhaps the worst of it. His mother went on cooking and cleaning. His father went on hauling grain to various millers as part of his contract with some local farmers. His sister studied and took care of Rachel. Rachel went on playing, and he, Reuven, practiced his violin. His playing had not suffered. Was this bad? He felt almost guilty for playing so well.

No one had held a second seder on the night of Muttle's capture. People were too scared. But now it was time for another holiday, Shavuot, the celebration of the Torah and the giving of the Ten Commandments. It was on Shavuot that children, when they were three years old, began their formal studies of Hebrew. That was when Reuven and Muttle had first met, almost twelve years before.

It was rumored that the village council made up lists of boys who could be drafted. They traded the lists for favors from the tsar's government—favors such as allowing their villages not to be burned, their families not to be murdered, their study houses and synagogues not to be destroyed. And everyone knew that there were Jew catchers, many of them Jewish, who snatched boys from the religious schools. There was a famous one from the Polish town of Orla who traveled far. His name was Lejb Tate, and he was said to be a strange and sadistic man, but a Jew nonetheless, who worked on a quota system for the tsar—so many Jewish boys delivered each year, for which he was paid handsomely. It was said that some village councils actually hired Lejb Tate secretly. On the councils there were scholarly rebbes. "Can you believe it, and they call themselves holy men?" Reuven's mother's strange mechanical voice came back to him. No, Reuven could not believe it for one minute.

Tonight those holy men, if they dared, would be praying in the synagogue all night long. Such was the custom. They would read from the Book of Prophets. They would read the Song at the Red Sea.

Reuven's mother and his sister were in the kitchen. Suddenly his father spoke. "Come, Reuven, we'll go to synagogue."

"Really, Papa?" Reuven looked up with surprise from the sheets of music he was studying before supper. Reuven saw his father looking at his mother's and Shriprinka's doughy fingers. The two women stopped what they were doing, but baby Rachel kept banging on a pot. For this, Reuven was thankful. He saw the resolve in his father's eyes. His father was no great scholar, but he was a Jew and he would not be bullied out of his beliefs, he would not be prevented from reading Torah on this evening.

There were more people in the synagogue than Reuven had expected, including his Uncle Chizor. Reuven and his father would not stay all night like many, but he was glad that they had arrived in time for the reading from Exodus of the miracle of the Red Sea.

He squeezed his eyes shut and pictured the scene. Reuven never imagined the sea as completely dry. There was just enough water to wade in, to splash, and kick up. There might be a ball the children could play with, and the sun would shine brightly. It would be very hot, but the splashing of the water would cool the people down. And Moses was not the big towering stern figure. He was kind, and he would speak to the children in a very soft voice, not the one that gave the commandments, but like a very gentle teacher, the likes of which Reuven had certainly never known. "Don't tarry, little ones," he would say. "There is still a far piece to travel. We must get on with it. I know you're all having fun, but splashing and frolicking in Red Sea puddles won't do just now. We'll never make it to the Promised Land at this rate. Hurry along, Zipporah. And you too, Jacob and Yitzak and Rachel and Reuven."

Miracles, Reuven thought. *Did anyone ever get tired of thinking about miracles?* When he grew up, he would like to compose an entire concerto. He would call it the Miracle Concerto for the Violin in D major.

Reuven and his family were in the back of the room. Up toward the front, he saw Reb Mendel and several of the village's most scholarly and holy men. Had any of these holy men been the ones to put the name of Isaac, the orphan, on the list? For the first time in a while, Reuven thought about poor Isaac. All these days he had grieved over the loss of Muttle, his best friend, and God knew the village had grieved over Muttle, their prize student. But had anyone given a thought to poor Isaac? Maybe they didn't deserve miracles.

Reuven's father nudged him in the ribs, the sign that they would be leaving. They followed Uncle Chizor out into the street. The evening was damp. A mist hung in the air outside the synagogue. Chizor took a small enamel box from his pocket, snapped it open, and got a pinch of snuff. Uncle Chizor was very fashionable, at least for Berischeva. He liked his snuff, and he ordered expensive brandy from Warsaw, and he had a large collection of books. Chizor often talked of moving to Vilna in Poland, and he always promised to take Reuven with him. Vilna was a center of music and culture and literature. There Reuven could study with the great violin teachers. As a tailor, Chizor made a good living. But he dreamed a rich man's dreams of drinking tea from magnificent silver samovars, served not in glasses but in porcelain teacups. He dreamed of leather-bound books and rich fabrics that he rarely touched in his everyday trade except, of course, when he tailored for the Baron Radzinsky.

"Well, boys!" Uncle Chizor always called them boys when it was just the three of them together. Reuven liked it. It made him feel as if he was part of a daring rugged little society. Not like these holy men, who could not see beyond their prayer books. "So we got away with it again!"

"Got away with what?" Reuven asked, but as soon as the question was out he felt stupid, for he had known the answer.

"Worshipping our God!" Chizor exclaimed. "What kind of a crazy place is this where you have to fear for your life to pray? My last time."

"What do you mean your last time? You giving up being a Jew?" Aaron Bloom asked.

"Don't be an idiot. Here, have a cigar." Chizor drew two out from his inside pocket. They stopped walking, and in the dim light of a street lamp that hung in the mist like a blurred pearl, he struck a match and lit the end of his brother's cigar and then his own. A rich dark smell swirled up in the dampness of the night. "Good, isn't it?" Aaron Bloom grunted his assent. "Havana."

"What?" Reuven and his father both said at once.

"Havana—cigars from Cuba. They're the best."

"Havana? Cuba? What's that?" Reuven was glad his father had asked and not him.

"An island! Cuba's an island. Havana is the capital."

"Where? The Black Sea?" Reuven blurted out.

Chizor smacked his forehead in disbelief. "No! The Caribbean."

"The Caribbean!" Both Reuven and his father said the word slowly. It had a music, a rhythm that Reuven had never before heard in any word. That it was the name of a sea was even better. "The Caribbean." He repeated the word slowly and perfectly.

"Yes, it is a sea just west of the Atlantic and south when you get to America. Yes, you turn left and then go down." Chizor was inscribing the air with the glowing tip of his cigar.

"Uncle Chizor, how did you get a cigar all the way from there?"

"The baron," both Aaron and Chizor said in unison. Of course it was the baron, who could provide everything from sheet music of Dvořák to cigars from a place called Cuba that floated in a sea that sang its name.

Aaron Bloom coughed, cleared his throat, and took a puff on his cigar. "So Chizzie, what is this about tonight being your last Shavuot service?"

Uncle Chizor stopped walking and held his glowing cigar aloft, as if to punctuate whatever came next. "Last in this *farshtinkener* country."

"*Farshtinkener* country? Chizzie. It is our home."

"Tell the tsar that, Aaron. And it's going to get worse."

"How so?" Reuven's father asked.

"New laws against Jews. We can't do this. We can't do that. We're no longer permitted to do business on Sunday or any of the Christian holidays. No more mortgages. And every day we hear about another pogrom. A supplier of damask I have dealt with for years now is forbidden to sell to me because I am a Jew. And that's the least of it. It's crazy. In what other country are Jews forced to serve in the army, and then that same army is given license to tear through their own villages and burn them? You know, I heard a story that in Bukova a mother cut off her boy's fingers so he would not be conscripted into the tsar's army." Reuven curled his hands in his pockets. He felt the calluses on his string hand against the softness of his palm.

Chizor looked up to the black sky swirling with stars, as if appealing to God. "So what's to be done? People either leave or get mad."

"What do you mean, Uncle? What do people do when they get mad?"

His uncle slid his eyes first toward Reuven's father, as if he was asking for permission.

"The Bund," Aaron said in a barely audible whisper.

"There are people," Chizor said quietly, "who stay but try to change things. These are very angry people; some call them revolutionaries."

"What do they do?" Reuven asked.

"They organize strikes, worker strikes, for better pay, better conditions. Some do sabotage."

"Sabotage? Sabotage what?"

"Weapons in the tsar's armories, maybe train tracks." Chizor flicked the ashes from his cigar. "But you see,

Reuven, I am not a revolutionary. I am a tailor. I have nobody to save except myself. I have anger. But I guess not enough to stay and turn the whole place upside down. And I have no patience. Yes, I am an impatient man. Very impatient, and that is why I choose to leave."

There was a fierceness in his uncle's voice, and the glow of the cigar now clamped between his teeth as he spoke cast a red shadow on his face. He looked quite angry to Reuven. His eyes were like two furious dashes. His black brows with their tufts of white slid together at steep angles. His mouth drew back in a weird grin, with the cigar still clamped between his square stained teeth. He looked like the devil, a *dybbuk* come to life on this little alley off Krupinsky. There was silence, an uncomfortable one. The smoke, the mist hung between them. Reuven bit his lip lightly.

"Uncle Chizor where are you going? Poland? Warsaw? Vilna?"

"Naw," he said roughly, then spat into the gutter. "They're still too close. No good for a Jew."

"Chizzie, are you going to America?" Aaron Bloom asked.

"Probably, but who knows? Maybe the Caribbean." He winked at Reuven. The old Uncle Chizor was back, not a trace of the *dybbuk*.

The three continued to walk up the hill of the narrow street that twisted like a corkscrew.

"New York, they say New York is good, Chizor," said Aaron.

"Ah New York—every tailor goes to New York. They got too many tailors there already. I'll go someplace where I can stand out. I don't know, maybe Canada, Montreal, Chicago, or someplace out west—the prairie—Minnesota."

"Minna—what?" Reuven asked

"Minnesota."

Reuven walked quietly as his father and his uncle continued to talk. Reuven wished his father would consider such a thing, but he never would. He knew his father. His father believed that Russia was their country. Their home. That they had a right to be here. Besides, his father had a wife and three children. Uncle Chizor had nothing but fine books and bottles of good brandy. He could leave tomorrow and take nothing, or perhaps a few books and a couple of bottles of brandy.

They walked on, talking and smoking, taking the long way home. The mist blew away; the night was black and starless. Reuven listened and wondered and thought. Even on this darkest night he could pick out the cats sliding across rooftops, the chimney pots that sometimes looked like hunched little men, the heap of rags that might be a beggar, the swift shadows that belonged to boys sneaking out of their bedroom windows. This was his home. He had learned how to sift the shadows of the Berischeva night, to pick out the blackness of a cat against the darkness of the evening, or the gray of a weathered fence from the dimness of a muddy yard. Why should they leave?

SIX

SPRING PASSED into summer, and before the green leaves turned to autumn gold, Uncle Chizor left for America. True to this word, he would not celebrate one more Jewish holiday in the *farshtinkener* country of Russia. Reuven had mastered the Bach concerto, and was even mastering the intricacies of the Dvořák, which had seemed deceptively simple. He had improved since that first night of seder when he had played it. He had learned that nothing was simple, and many things were deceptive.

But not a day went by that Reuven did not think of Muttle, and now Uncle Chizor was gone too. Reuven had been thinking of him often in the three weeks since he had gone. He sat by the river now and thought about the deception of things, of appearances, of people, of music, of holiness, of words, and of the river itself, where he had last spoken with Muttle five months before. It was still unbelievable, unacceptable, that those words would be the last that he and Muttle would ever exchange. How placid the river had been on that day. How placid it was on this day. Yet Reuven knew that there was a strong current. It was a dangerous river. Here at this very spot the current might not be so strong, but one hundred meters down it grew fierce. Still one would never know, for it never showed on the surface because the river was so deep. Anyone weighing under thirty-five kilos had no chance if he or she were to fall in.

How many children had been sucked away by this river? Too many. Yet this was the very river that he had run to on the night Rachel was born for cold water. This river, which sucked away life, had caused her to breathe, to yowl, to turn pink and lively. Maybe it wasn't deceptions but contradictions that filled life. Maybe in order to begin to understand the world, one had to begin to accept contradictions as a fact. But was it a contradiction or a deception now that the high holy days of Rosh Hashanah and Yom Kippur had passed? There had been no pogroms, no violence, no rumors of harassment from other villages. Why were they being left alone by the tsar and the Cossacks, who loved to kill and kidnap on the holidays?

Tonight was the first night of Sukkoth, the harvest festival. It would be the first time they had built the sukkah hut without Uncle Chizor. For seven days they would have their meals in the outdoor little lean-to constructed against the side of their house. It would be made from wooden planks, branches, and old doors that they had kept over the years just for this structure. Sometimes Reuven had slept out in the sukkah with Muttle and through the spindly tree limbs they had watched the stars all night long.

But it's not the same, not without Uncle Chizor, not without Muttle.

These thoughts stayed with Reuven, clung to him,

and would not free him long after he had left the river and gone home.

"Reuven, you don't like the noodle kugel?" his mother said. "Reuven! Reuven! You're a million miles away."

"You going deaf?" his father said. "Not good for a musician to be deaf—except Beethoven. He seemed to do all right."

"What?" Reuven suddenly was aware that all of his family was looking at him and that they had been speaking to him.

"You're a million miles away, I say. You haven't touched your food. You're not feeling well?" his mother asked.

"No, I'm fine, Mama," Reuven said. But she was right. He had been a million miles away. He had been looking through the pine boughs of the sukkah roof at the stars, the same ones that were shining now on Uncle Chizor, who was maybe in the middle of the Atlantic Ocean. Or maybe they were shining on Muttle, and only God knew where Muttle was. If the same stars shone over every place and everyone, why . . . why . . . But his mind could barely finish the thought. Why was Uncle Chizor having to leave this *farshtinkener* country and why had Muttle been snatched by the tsar?

Rachel crawled onto his lap. She seemed to know that he was thinking about the stars. Perhaps she had watched him looking through the pine boughs of the sukkah roof.

"Up! Up!" She pointed at the roof. She wanted

him to hold her up so she could touch the branches. "Up! Up!"

Reuven raised her in his arms and let her touch the pine branches. She reached out and then suddenly she stopped and pointed her finger right through the bristles.

"Moon . . . piece of moon," she said quite clearly.

They could hardly believe their ears.

"What's that, Rachel?" Reuven asked. "What did you just say? What's that?" He pointed his own finger right through the branches at the sliver of moon sailing overhead.

"Moon . . . piece of moon," she repeated.

They all exclaimed with wonder. The child was barely sixteen months old. She had not just spoken the word *moon* but was so smart that she recognized it as a piece of the moon and not the whole.

"Maybe you'll grow up to be an astronomer!" Shriprinka cried with delight, and chucked Rachel under her chin. "Or a mathematician."

Reuven was excited too, until it suddenly dawned on him that she would be none of these things if she grew up in Russia. There was no place for Jewish astronomers, let alone women who were Jewish astronomers, mathematicians, or writers. *In fact,* Reuven thought as he raised her once more to touch the roof, *what is the point of growing up at all in Russia?* His uncle had been right.

That was the night when Reuven stopped playing his violin.

SEVEN

IT HAD taken the rest of autumn for the calluses on Reuven's string fingers to soften, then disappear almost entirely. Now it was winter. A stinging cold had set in, and as Reuven went out to the woodpile with a wheelbarrow to load up with logs for the stove, he had to blow on his hands to keep them warm. Had the calluses, he wondered, insulated his skin? It was certainly true that the wood felt rougher. He paused and looked at his hands. They were no longer the hands of a violinist. Odd, he thought, how those thick patches of rough skin that made it so easy for him to finger the strings with just the right pressure could vanish, and yet the music still lingered in his head.

In the beginning, his family questioned him. But Reuven was unwavering. Soon they stopped asking him if or when he would play again. It didn't matter, however. For they didn't have to say anything out loud. They asked a thousand times a day in their own way. His father would pull out his watch every afternoon at the time Reuven had gone to Herschel's for his lesson and then look from it, as if to say, *Why are you still here?*

His mother, who was not exactly musically gifted, had taken to humming disjointed snatches of the pieces she had remembered Reuven practicing. And Shriprinka, more on key, would also hum. Rachel had taken a more direct approach. She toddled over to where Reuven's violin case rested on a shelf and pounded her chubby fist on it, then looked at Reuven. He merely walked over and, feeling every eye in the room on him, put it on a higher shelf.

"Not now," he had said firmly to his baby sister. The unspoken word *When?* seethed in the air.

"All right, enough is enough!" Herschel stood at the foot of Reuven's bed. Herschel's father, Reb Itchel, was there as well. Reuven blinked. It was late. The sun was up.

"What's he doing here?" Reuven asked, nodding toward Reb Itchel.

"You need all the help you can get, young man. I'll bring the cursed tsar in here if I have to, in order to get you out of bed." He held up the violin, which Reuven had not touched in several months. "You see this? This is what you were born to do. This is your gift. You must play."

Then Reb Itchel muttered an old Yiddish phrase. *"Az me redt tsu im, is azoy vi me redt tsu a toyte vantz."* Talking to him is like talking to a dead bedbug.

"Oh, you're some help, Papa! You're supposed to be praying for this stupid boy."

"Oh!" said the old rebbe, suddenly remembering his role. He began to rock back and forth in prayer. Reuven's eyes fixed on the little wisp of the white beard. He had once played Bach while watching the beard keep the rhythm and quiver to the vibrato.

Herschel continued. "I've had enough of your parents' thoughts on this subject. 'Oh, go easy. He will come back to it. He is just a boy.' No, enough is enough. You be at my house tomorrow. We begin with the Dvořák. Also, be ready with the Beethoven Romance in G major, and you take a look at the *Kreutzer Sonata*. You were making a real mess out of that one last time."

Herschel pulled on his father's shoulder. "We're going now and leaving this miserable piece of a boy to his thoughts." Just as he was about to walk out the door, he turned. "By the way, tomorrow evening Hanukkah starts. Hanukkah is a time for miracles. So it would be a miracle if you could play the first four measures of that Dvořák with anything approaching subtlety after so much time with no practice."

From his bed, Reuven could see the river. The sunlight glinted off its still surface. Then something odd happened. There were radiating glints of light on the water, as if a stone had been skipped across. It seemed as if an invisible hand had tossed an invisible stone. And then Muttle's words came back to Reuven: "You carry the music. I carry the words."

Reuven thought Herschel and Reb Itchel had gone, but suddenly he saw a little wisp of white drifting into his side vision. Reb Itchel had leaned back into the room and fixed Reuven in the pale light of his nearly translucent eyes. Had the rebbe made that stone skip across the river? Was this a miracle or a prayer? Then Reb Itchel seemed to whirl out in the wake of his very angry son.

Reuven got out of bed and stood barefoot in his pajamas. He looked at his fingers and wondered how long it would take for the calluses to come back. He picked up the violin. The first sheet of the *Kreutzer Sonata* was out on a low chest. He began. It sounded as if mice were gnawing on the strings. Rachel peeked around the corner now. She had a perplexed look on her face. *In another second she will be sticking her fingers in her ears*, Reuven thought. *It's going to take more than a miracle.*

The next day Reuven stood in Herschel's cottage in the middle of the floor. He was trying his best with the Dvořák. It was a worse mess than the *Kreutzer Sonata*, but Herschel was patient. More patient than usual. Reuven knew it was simply because he was back.

"You're trying too hard," Herschel said. "Relax. Try not to think so hard about each note. Think in phrases. The notes will gather, just like those snowflakes out there."

It had begun snowing midway through his lesson, and Reuven could see that the corners of the window-panes were collecting the snow in little sweeps. He imagined the hills outside of town where he and Muttle used to take their sleds. The first snows often came during Hanukkah, and by the end of the holiday week, he and Muttle could usually count on at least one or two days of good sledding. That is what he thought about now. Sledding. The sting of the cold air on his cheeks. There was that sound of the snow on the runners. Snowflakes now smeared the sky. The line of trees marking the edge of the forest became a solid dark band.

The lesson ended better than it had begun. As Reuven left Herschel's house, he wondered how he ever could have thought about giving up the violin. In the months that he had stopped playing, had anything improved? No, nothing at all. He had felt strange, almost disoriented. Although life in Russia for a Jew was mean and hard, for Reuven life without music was death. Now he felt alive again, as the snowflakes swirled about him.

The ferocity of the storm had increased. Reb Mendel's house was like a dim shadow against the sky. Light was leaking out of this day faster than Reuven could walk against the biting wind. He must hurry so he could be home in time to light the first candle in the menorah. The darkness gathered around him as he ran toward the village. There was no moon. The first night of Hanukkah was always moonless. There was never supposed to be a moon, for this was a holiday about the destruction of light when the Syrians entered the temple in Jerusalem and defiled the oil for the lamps. And then there was the miracle of light when the oil, only enough for one night, burned for eight days. Hanukkah was about light and miracles.

Tonight they would light the first candle, tomorrow another, and then another, and another, until the menorah glowed with nine candles, including the *shammes*, the candle by which all the others were lit. Reuven's family always set the menorah in the window. Each night as the number of candles increased, the reflections in the window multiplied even more because of the optical tricks of the glass, especially on a cold snowy night when the glass was etched with frost trees, which provided even more surfaces for reflections. Uncle Chizor had explained this to him—the mathematics of optics and light and reflection. But Reuven found that it was better to think about the miracle rather than about the numbers, in the same way that Herschel had told him to think about the phrase rather than the individual notes.

He stomped his feet before going through the door.

"Good lesson?" His father looked up from his account books.

"Good lesson, Papa, but I need to practice."

"You play me something just a little. The Dvořák, maybe?"

"All right, Papa, but I am still rusty. Just a few measures." Reuven took out his violin, tucked it under his chin, closed his eyes, and remembered the snowflakes gathering in little sweeps in Herschel's window.

"Aah." His father sighed with pleasure at the end of the first five measures. His face broke into a wide grin.

The smell of latkes swirled through the air. Reuven walked over to the stove, where his mother was frying the grated-up potatoes into patties.

"No snitching," she said as she saw Reuven's hand reach for one of the crisp golden pancakes on the warming platter at the edge of the stove top. "Make yourself useful. Sprinkle some sugar on those. This is my last batch, then we'll light the candles, and then we'll eat."

"How come she gets one?" Reuven said, pointing at Rachel, who was sitting on the floor happily munching away on a latke.

"Because she is a nineteen-month-old baby and she has been whining all day. I think she is coming down with an earache. And it was either give her a latke or spank her. Latkes work better," Bathshepa said matter-of-factly. Her face was red from the heat of the stove.

Ten minutes later Reuven, Shriprinka, Rachel, and their parents stood in front of the window where the menorah had been placed. They were ready to recite the blessing of the first of the Hanukkah lights. After lighting the first candle, they would receive their Hanukkah gelt—a few kopeks, which Reuven might use to rent a book from the storybook man. Perhaps he could persuade Shirprinka to use her gelt for a book as well. Rachel, instead of money, would receive a little wool mouse her mother had knitted. Then they would play the chance game dreidel with the wooden tops their father had carved for them years before. Then they would eat more latkes, and their mother would say as she always did, "I think I used too much oil in that last batch."

Reuven was thinking of all this as his mother lit the candle and they began to recite the blessing. *"Baruch atah Adonai, Eloheinu melech ha'olam, asher kidshanu b'mitzvotav, v'tzivanu l'hadlik ner shel Chanukah."* Praised are you, Lord our God, ruler of the universe, who has sanctified our lives through His commandments, commanding us to kindle the Hanukkah lights.

The reflection of the candle flared in the window, and then suddenly there was a blur outside, a white terrified face. A wild knocking at the door. Who could it be at this hour? Reuven went to the door. It was Yitzak, the boy from down the street. He was no more than ten, but small for his age.

"Hide!" he screamed. "Hide!"

"What's this?" Reuven's father came to the door.

"The tsar, his troops, they just torched Pecorchova," Yitzak said.

"Pecorchova!" they all gasped. Pecorchova was the nearest village, less than five miles away.

"Reuven, you must hide. I must go," Yitzak gasped the words.

Bathshepa's hands raked through her hair. Rachel began to cry. The last thing that Reuven clearly remembered was the reflection of the flickering candle lights in the pane of the window. Then his parents were stuffing him down the potato hole. He heard the thunk of the plank of wood being set in the floor. Then all was darkness.

He had not been in the hole for more than a few minutes when he heard the pounding of horses' hooves and rough loud voices. He knew those voices spoke Russian, and although Reuven's first language was Yiddish, he understood Russian. But he could not quite make out what they were saying. Then there was a crash, and the words came very clearly.

"Search the house for any young males. You, old man, take a seat. You, woman, get me your chickens, every single one. No hiding." Reuven heard the backyard door shut as his mother went out to fetch the chickens they kept in the pen.

Next there was a terrible cacophony of squawking chickens mixed with the wails of Rachel and the shrieks of his mother. A gruff "no! no!" he knew was his father's voice. Then a terrible cry split the air. It was all Reuven could do to remain in the hole. How could he be here, crouched like a rat in the darkness when his mother, father, two sisters . . . God only knew what was happening to them. And then sudden quiet. He did not even remember hearing the stomp of the soldiers' boots as they left. There was only a deathly stillness, and finally a voice. It was Rachel. "Papa! Papa!" she screamed.

Someone was shifting the plank above his head. A crack of light began to dance over his knees. Shriprinka's face was white and her eyes, as wide and dark as river stones, looked down.

"You can come out now, for a little while we think. We think they have gone for a while."

He lifted himself from the hole. The heel of his hand skidded on something warm and wet. He knew instantly it was blood, and then he looked at his father, who sat collapsed on a chair, holding a blanket to one side of his head.

"They cut off his ear," Bathshepa said in a trembling voice. "I got part of it here. Maybe we send for the doctor. Maybe he can sew it back on."

"No! No!" Aaron Bloom waved her off. "Let them have my ear."

Reuven wanted to cry, *Let them have your ear, Papa? Your ear? Your ear into which I poured those measures of music less than an hour ago. With no ear, how do you hear music? They tear your ear, they break our song.* But Reuven was too stunned to say anything. He merely stood with his hand covering his mouth. He did not even notice the wreck the Cossack soldiers had left. Tables upturned. Latkes on the floor. Chicken feathers still drifting through the air. The oddest thing of all was that the menorah still stood in the window with its candles burning. Reuven turned around slowly, looking for the silver Shabbat candlesticks.

"They stole the candlesticks," said his mother, reading his mind. The candlesticks were real silver. The menorah was only plated silver.

"How did they know the difference between the candlesticks and the menorah?" Reuven wondered aloud.

"Oh, some of these Cossacks come from very fine homes. You know, raised properly. They know the difference between real silver and plate," his mother said as she looked straight down at the floor where a bloody pulp that had once been an ear lay. It was the same mechanical voice that Reuven had heard on the night they had snatched Muttle—colorless, without anger, as if his mother were a machine.

∾ EIGHT ∾

"BARUCH ATAH Adonai, Eloheinu melech ha'olam, asher kidshanu b'mitzvotav, v'tzivanu l'hadlik ner shel Chanukah."

From the thick darkness of the potato hole, Reuven heard his family recite the blessing of the Hanukkah lights now for the fifth time. It was the fifth night of Hanukkah. He had spent most of every night and every day in the potato hole. The entire village had lived in abject terror now for five days. There was no choice except to hide Reuven, for an order had gone out to scour the village of Berischeva for males twelve years and older. Many had tried to flee into the woods, but they were caught, because the countryside crawled with Cossacks.

The commandant of the eighth division of the tsar's army had decided to make his headquarters in Berischeva. The women had been ordered to bake bread for the troops. Every lamb, every chicken had been slaughtered. Violence and disorder reigned. From the darkness of his own private hell, Reuven could not see the hell above. But he could hear and he could smell, and it was a pungent odor of scorched wood, smoldering cottages, and baking bread that hung over the village. Any family that would not comply or that was suspected of holding out in any way was burned out of their home. From his hole, he heard it all. He listened to his mother's soothing voice as she tended to his father's injury, replacing the bandages that covered the place where his ear had been. Although it must have hurt, his father never once cried out in pain. He heard the neighbor women and the old men come by with the latest gossip and rumor—the tsar's army plans to march into Austria and take over the throne of the Austrian king, the Hapsburg throne. The tsar's army will march all the way to Germany and kill the kaiser. The tsar's army will invade Turkey, and the tsar and the tsarina will have themselves crowned emperor and empress of the Ottoman Empire.

The only blessing, if one could call it that, was that Rachel's earache had worsened, and to ease the pain, Reuven's parents had been giving her sleeping draughts. She was kept sufficiently quiet and groggy so that she did not go looking for her brother. Perhaps she had completely forgotten that he was in the potato hole. Once she whimpered for him and was told he was at his violin lesson. Reuven practically laughed out loud when he heard this.

Although it could not be said that he had grown used to the darkness, he had done something to make the hole became somewhat more bearable. He had learned to fill it with his own imagination. Reuven furnished it with pictures of his family in their daily life. And though their daily life was gripped with terror, Aaron and Bathshepa Bloom had insisted that they light the Hanukkah candles every night.

"It takes courage to receive a miracle. And besides, Hanukkah is not just about light and miracles. It is about freedom. It is about being a Jew despite all—despite the Syrians one thousand years ago, despite the tsar now. It is the weak against the mighty. We are not simply Jewish shtetl people, we are resisters in the tradition of Judas Maccabee, Judas the Hammer with his renegade soldiers in the hills outside of Jerusalem. They were weak. They were poor farmers, and yet after three years, they regained the temple from the very Syrians who had defiled it, and they won. That was not a miracle, not like the oil that lasted for eight days. It was the victory of faith and dedication and courage. No courage, no miracles. You think the Red Sea would have parted if the people hadn't had the *chutzpah* to thumb their noses at the pharaoh and get up off their tokheses and leave?"

This is what Aaron Bloom would say every night just before they lit the candles.

On the sixth night of Hanukkah as his family chanted the blessing of the lights, Reuven could picture them standing there—Shriprinka, Mama, Papa, baby Rachel, thankfully, asleep in her crib. He could even imagine the lights reflected in the blackness of the windows. Were there frost trees on the glass tonight? Perhaps not, for it had begun to rain earlier. So that would mean the reflections of the lights would slide into shimmering liquid shapes. They would dance across the wet windowpanes like flames, like the light of a *dybbuk's* face, like . . . like, oh where was Uncle Chizor on this night? Reuven could see the thick eyebrows with their tufts of white dancing up and down through the smoke of his Cuban cigar. Maybe he had gone to Cuba, to the city of Havana. Or was he in that frozen north place, the place of the lakes like claws that he had once shown Reuven on the map in his library? What funny thoughts he had here in the darkness. And the thoughts were laced with music, all the beautiful music he had learned to play since he was six years old—the Brahms, the Beethoven, the Bach. The music streamed through him, through the darkness. It filled his being until his soul sang and he felt in his own way as powerful as Judas the Hammer hiding out in the Judean Hills of Jerusalem. These were his Judean Hills—this darkness, this hole.

✦ ✦ ✦

The next day, Reuven was dozing when he heard excited voices above him. It was Shriprinka.

"Mama! Papa!" She had just returned from the marketplace. "They are saying that the women and the children shall be taken out to the forest and shot if all the boys in Berischeva are not given up in the next twenty-four hours."

"What?" Reuven's father asked.

"Yes, it is true," said another voice. Reuven recognized it as Beryl, Shriprinka's good friend. "They know many families are still hiding sons."

"Oh my God!" moaned his mother. "What are we to do?"

"We must leave," said his father. "We must leave separately from Reuven. We shall go to Zarichka and then to Vilna. It will be safe. And then from there . . . Yes, yes, I guess America."

America! Reuven could hardly believe his ears. The map he had studied at Uncle Chizor's library now danced in his imagination. The claw lakes, called the Great Lakes, sparkled fiercely. He could picture it all: the thin blue thread called the St. Lawrence River, the sausage named Florida, Minnesota, the shining sea on the far edge of the map.

Reuven heard the door close as Beryl left. He heard his father walking toward the potato hole, hopefully to tell him what to do. Where to meet in Vilna, for they would not be able to meet up in Zarichka. It would be unsafe, but Vilna would be good. Vilna even had a music academy. Perhaps they would meet there. First his father spoke to his mother. Reuven heard him talking about a distant cousin in Vilna. This was news to Reuven. A cousin named Lovotz Sperling, a book dealer. Then his mother and father and Shriprinka began speaking in terse sentences.

"Wrap up some diapers for the baby . . . We take nothing but the clothes on our backs . . . A loaf of bread . . . Coins, sew the coins into the hems of your skirts . . . Rachel's medicine . . . Sturdy shoes . . . your sturdiest shoes."

And then his father was standing very near the potato hole. He dared not uncover it. He spoke rapidly. The words were directed to Reuven, who crouched with his chin to his knees and listened.

"Lovotz Sperling, off Szeroka Street. It's an alley, really. I forget the name. Not far from the great synagogue."

Suddenly a great clattering. Things were crashing. Reuven heard a horse's excited snorting and hooves pounding. Hooves right in the house! On the planks of their own floor! Above the potato hole, a deafening clatter and thunder. Dirt was shaking down. He heard screaming.

"Don't take him! Don't take him!"

A shot tore through the screams, then another and another. A large splinter of wood was blasted from the plank covering the potato hole, and suddenly a wedge of light dropped into the darkness. Reuven froze. He dared not breathe. Above he heard a soft moan near the potato hole. He rose slightly so he could peer through the slot that had been shot away. Reuven opened his eyes in horror. Shriprinka lay inches from him. There was a gaping wound in her neck, from which blood poured. The shiny boots of a Cossack stepped neatly over her. Reuven saw a hand reach down. Was the soldier going to help her? The hand took out a pistol from a leg holster. Reuven watched, transfixed. It was one seamless movement. The hand drew the trigger and shot his sister in the chest. The other hand reached for Reuven's violin. A slice of lamplight cut across Reuven's face, then darkness filled his brain and everything was quiet. Very quiet.

NINE

REUVEN HAD no notion of time. It could have been hours since his sister's murder, or days, or maybe just minutes. It was as if he had been wrapped in an all-enveloping numbness. He felt neither cold nor hunger nor loss nor outrage nor despair. He could not cry, but he was suddenly aware of a little cry coming from someone else, a whimpering that seemed to scratch at the numbness of the chamber that sealed him off from all feeling. He blinked. The light that fell through the slot was not lamplight, but natural light from a window. An entire night must have passed. It was a new day. The whimpering sound pulled him inexorably toward it.

Like a fish pulled from the sea, Reuven felt himself being reeled out of his hole. He was beyond fear; he was beyond hope. For the first time in a week he stood up to his full height in the light of day. Something lay on the floor twisted and caked with blood. *This is not Shriprinka.* The words thundered in his head. No, not his sister! He refused to believe that. He could not touch her. If he touched her, he would have to believe. But he could not leave her like this. He took a tapestry that Uncle Chizor had given them. It had been torn off the wall, and he now spread it over Shriprinka's body.

No sooner had he done that then there was the whimpering sound again, then a cry. A loud insistent cry. Where was that coming from? Everything was turned topsy-turvy. Tables upended, bed mattresses ripped open. His mother's sewing machine lay smashed in the fireplace, and the big wardrobe that his father had taken the door off and built a few shelves in for their few books and dishes was facedown on the floor. This was where the whimpering was coming from.

Reuven stood and looked down at the back side of the wardrobe. Another cry.

"Rachel?"

This must be the miracle, Reuven thought as he lifted the heavy wardrobe and discovered Rachel in her crib. She raised her arms to Reuven. Her face was smeared with tears and snot. But she was alive! The huge crash he had heard the night before had been the wardrobe falling over. Falling over so precisely it had simply dropped like an enormous box over Rachel's small crib, sealing her off from the violence of the slaughter. And it had been a slaughter. Shriprinka was dead. He could see the bodies of his father and mother through the doorway of the cottage, for there was no longer a door. It had been torn off. Beyond them, other bodies lay in the street. Several houses had been burned to the ground. By some miracle, theirs had been spared, or else he and Rachel would have never found themselves alive on this morning, the last day of Hanukkah.

Rachel was remarkably well, considering that she had spent the last fourteen hours in a coffinlike box. The sleeping draught they had given her must have worked very well. She was hungry and she was frightened. Her little mouth stretched into an enormous, lopsided, dark O as she howled for her mama. It was a din of rage, and her eyes seemed to slide with terror. Then she looked at her brother as if to say, *Fix this. I am the baby! Just a baby. Feed me!* And Reuven realized that it was all up to him now. Her life depended on him. Him alone. There was no one to help them. There were only people out there who could kill them.

And then it suddenly struck Reuven that it was very possible that he and Rachel were the only living things left in Berischeva. He had not heard a dog bark, a horse whinny, a chicken cluck. He had not heard the voices of any humans. He had not even heard a footstep in the street. The stillness began to creep into him, settle in him like mist. The Cossacks were gone and everybody else was dead. This he knew. Therefore, at this moment he and Rachel were in no immediate danger, but he had to make plans. Careful small plans. He could proceed only step by step. His first problem was how to prevent

Rachel from seeing the dead bodies of their parents and Shriprinka. This made burying them impossible. He knew it was terrible to leave them like this, but what choice did he have? His duty was to the living, his little sister.

Then the first step of a small plan took shape in his brain. He and Rachel would leave by the back door. But they could not leave in the light of day, could they? The Cossacks might be just outside the village. And yet if they waited here, Rachel might discover Shriprinka under the tapestry or run out the front door. She was already squirming in his lap. They would have to leave now. He would just have to be very careful. He sat staring at one of the immense woven baskets that his father used for transporting grain to the miller. It gave him an idea. Rachel could easily fit into the basket. If he strapped it to his back and then wrapped his head up with scarves and wore a skirt of his mother's—there was one flung over in a corner—from a distance, he might look like one of the old Russian peasant women going to market. Anything was better than looking like what he was—a nearly sixteen-year-old Jewish boy, muscular and fit for the tsar's army.

Reuven told Rachel to sit very still, that he was going to show her something funny. He had managed to find her a hunk of cheese and some bread, which seemed to satisfy her for now. He went and put on his mother's skirt. Rachel looked at him curiously, her face slipping to an expression halfway between a laugh and a cry. Next he found some of his mother's scarves and wrapped them around his head just like the babushkas the Russia peasant women wore. Rachel pointed. The corners of her mouth crinkled into a tentative smile.

"Yes, aren't I funny? You can call me Miriam, or Tovah, or . . ." Another odd expression seemed to play across her face. *She's trying to figure this out,* Reuven thought.

"Mama!" Rachel pointed her finger again and giggled a bit.

"Yes, Mama." Reuven whispered the words so softly only he could hear them.

"Mama!" It began as a whimper, a plea. But then her face slid into that awful grimace. The little mouth began to stretch into the dark hole that seemed to blot out her features. It was almost as if she were swallowing herself.

"Mama! Mama!"

The entire house seemed to shake with the single word. Now Rachel was standing up and stomping her little feet. Her face, turning red, was contorted into a horrid mask. Suddenly it was illuminated by a shaft of brilliant sunlight that flooded through the two small windows of the house. God, she looked like a baby *dybbuk*. It was as if a tiny evil spirit had taken her over. He had to get her out of here. She was toddling toward the doorway. Reuven lunged for her as she began to run off. In one swoop he put her in the big basket and slung it up onto his back. Now Rachel whooped with glee. This was the greatest fun! Whoever heard of riding in Papa's wheat basket?

They were out the door, through the muddy backyard. One large open field to cross and then they would be at the edge of the woods. They could lose themselves in the dense shadows of the trees. There they would wait until dark, when it would be safer to travel.

As soon as they had gotten beyond the village, somehow Rachel had sensed that her mama and papa were gone. Carrying her on his back, Reuven could almost feel her stiffen through the basket. A cry so wrenching and so enormous came from her that it stunned Reuven. He could hardly believe that a body so small could make such a sound. She cried and cried and cried and then, finally exhausted, she fell asleep in the basket.

It grew colder as the afternoon wore on. Rachel awoke and began to squirm in the basket. He knew he had to get into the woods and build a fire to warm them. Reuven had remembered to throw the rest of the bread and cheese into the basket with Rachel, along with a box of matches, but he had forgotten diapers. This thought first struck him as he lifted Rachel from the basket in the woods and set her down by the stream where they had come to rest.

"Phew! Rachel! You stink."

Rachel giggled. The giggle startled Reuven. It was a relief. Had she momentarily forgotten this sudden rearrangement of her world? Had the gaping hole somehow closed? This gave Reuven an idea. Perhaps he could make her believe that they were on some wonderful, funny adventure. Yes, a funny game where he dressed up like a little old lady and she rode in a grain basket. The problem was that this little old lady didn't know the first thing about changing a diaper, even if "she" had had a fresh one. He supposed he could spare one of the scarves from his babushka if it were absolutely necessary.

Two seconds later he decided it was absolutely necessary.

"Come here, Rachel. We've got to change your diaper."

Somehow, Reuven managed to do this. He tried to tie the nappy knots the way they had been. He took the dirty nappy and rinsed it in the stream. He cleaned Rachel's dirty bottom with snow, which made her squeal but not really cry.

Darkness on this short December day had begun to fall by midafternoon. In another hour it would be safe for them to travel, but where would they be going? All the way to Vilna, he supposed. But that would take days. It was maybe one hundred miles from their little village in the Pale. Hadn't Reuven heard somewhere that there was a priest in Posva who befriended Jews? Posva was not that far. Maybe two or three days' travel from where they were. And once in Posva, maybe another two days to Vilna.

What choice did they have?

The stubble of the fields turned to gold in the last rays of the setting sun. Crouched in the shadows of the woods, Reuven and Rachel looked across the field to Berischeva. Some of the houses were still smoldering, and curls of smoke and ash rose in the air hanging over the village like a dark calligraphy. He could actually pick out the chimney of their house, the house where his mother and father and older sister lay dead. The setting sun seemed to break on the horizon like a bloodied egg. The sky flared, and it began to snow lightly. The flakes came down slowly, each spinning in a dance of its own making against the blood-streaked orange of the sky.

The snowflakes seemed to grow larger, move more slowly, and it was almost as if he could see their intricate crystal pattern, white and beautiful against the fiery red sky. He had seen their bloodied bodies, but it was only now that Reuven finally realized that he would never see his parents and older sister again. Minyans, gatherings of at least ten men, were required for prayers of mourning. There was only himself and Rachel, but Reuven's lips began to move around the barely whispered words of a Jewish prayer.

"In the flight of a bird, we shall remember them. In the stirring of a leaf, we shall remember them. In the first blades of grass after a long winter, we shall remember them. In the rising of the sun and in its going down, we shall remember them. . . . As long as we live they too shall live for now they are a part of us, as we remember them."

His eyes streamed with tears, and even though the Cossack had walked off with his violin, it seemed as though some ineffable part of the instrument had been left behind. With it came the ghosts of the Cerutis, the violin makers from Cremona. They were his minyan. The soul of the violin rested now somewhere deep within him. It had joined with his own soul to help him chant these prayers of loss and grief for his mother and father and Shriprinka and yes, for Herschel and Reb Itchel, for they undoubtedly lay dead as well. But then the darkness seeped over the land and it was time to leave. The crooked old lady with her huge bundle dissolved into the snowy night.

TEN

THE COALS in the brazier glowed as bright as oranges. The priest urged them to move closer.

"But not too close, for the baby. Babies' skin is so much more delicate than ours," he said.

The priest stroked Rachel's cheek and then patted his own, which was plump and smooth. Reuven thought his skin looked very delicate, for a grown-up.

They had arrived at the priest's house a few hours before, in the late afternoon. It had taken them a day longer to get to Posva than he had anticipated, and by the time they got there they were cold and very hungry. But at least Rachel's earache had gone away. In the three days they had been on the road, they had seen half a dozen villages like Berischeva that had been destroyed by the tsar's troops. Their bread and cheese had given out a day and a half earlier. They had passed an orchard, and by digging in the deep snowdrifts, they had collected some old withered apples from beneath the trees. Even the worms had deserted these apples, and not much fruit was left, but Reuven and Rachel ate them anyway.

Now they had already been fed a bowl of cabbage soup and bread with pickled herring, in front of the fire. Reuven knew that they must be careful. After eating so little over the past few days, they could make themselves sick. But the food kept coming. The priest sipped a cherry liquor that he said aided his digestion, and from the looks of what the servant was setting on the table, he would need it. A roast chicken and rolled veal breast stuffed with vegetables, steaming pots of potatoes, and a fish fillet baked in a clear jelly.

"Are we almost ready, Bozieka?" the priest asked.

The servant, a corpulent lady with a face the color of raw meat and glistening with perspiration, nodded and made a grunting sound as she set down the last bowl.

"Come, children," he said.

Reuven took Rachel's hand and followed the priest to the table. It was spread with a delicately embroidered cloth, gleaming silver bowls, and platters laden with food. Rachel's eyes were wide with wonder. Reuven could not help but think it was a lot better business being a priest than a rabbi. He had never seen a rabbi's table so laden.

The priest poured them a bit of wine in their cups. Reuven did not really want wine, but he felt it would be impolite to refuse. The priest was already raising his glass.

"A toast to our guests, Bozieka," he said.

Bozieka had no glass, but her lips moved in a tight

little smile. Her mouth was very small for her large face and it gave the appearance of having been stitched on like that of a rag doll. *If she smiles too much, the stitches might rip,* Reuven thought. Her eyes were pale, and Reuven could not tell if they were brown or gray or perhaps green. They seemed diluted like weak tea. She had no eyebrows but had drawn two highly arched curves above her eyes with a black pencil.

The priest bowed his head to give a blessing. Reuven did as well.

When he was finished, the priest looked up. "So you say Berischeva is ruined?"

"Yes, sir, and so is Ru'ov and Pecorchova and . . ." Reuven's voice dwindled off.

"You speak good Russian. Where did you learn?"

"There is an academy"—Reuven paused—"or there *was* an academy in my village. Small, but one teacher came from St. Petersburg and another came from Moscow. So we learned Russian."

"Now tell me once more . . . where are you heading?"

Reuven had not told him the first time. For some reason he did not want to say exactly where he was going. If the soldiers came to question the priest, it could be dangerous for him. For the priest's own sake it might be better if he did not know.

"We are to join relatives."

"And where might these relatives be?"

"Grodno."

Reuven didn't know why he had said Grodno so quickly. It was as if his tongue was not his own for a brief instant.

"Ah, Grodno. Yes, there are many Jews in Grodno. They have it a bit easier, I think. Here, have some more beets. Bozieka is the master beet pickler, or should I say the mistress of beet pickling." He looked at the servant, who stood by at attention.

"The baby doesn't eat much," Bozieka said.

"Oh, you must realize that it is hard for us to eat a lot after eating so little. It is better for us to go a bit easy," Reuven replied. Rachel was playing with a bean on her plate. Bozieka sniffed. Reuven was not sure if it was a sniff of disapproval or agreement.

"Ah, but you must save a little room for Bozieka's pastries. They are superb," said the priest.

A few minutes later, Bozieka brought in a tray of pastries. There were tiny frosted cakes and sugared nuts and little cream-filled tarts. Reuven noticed a small tail of cream in the corner of Bozieka's mouth. She must have eaten one in the kitchen. The priest was piling their plates with samples of each. There was no way he could eat this, and he prayed that Rachel, who was pointing excitedly at the fancifully glazed cakes, would take one bite and be satisfied.

"Aah, my little pumpkin, you like those pretty cakes," said the priest. "Here, have two."

Reuven suddenly wanted to get away from the table. He yawned, which he knew was rude, but perhaps this would be a hint.

"You are both tired. Do you want to take a pot of tea up to bed along with some of these cakes?" asked the priest.

"Oh that is very kind of you, sir," said Reuven.

"And when you leave tomorrow, we shall have a packet of food for that big basket of yours. It will fit with you, won't it?" He reached over and gave Rachel's cheek a playful pinch. Rachel tucked her chin down into her collar.

"Bozieka, show the children to their bedchamber. And oh, don't forget the plate of cookies and cakes."

They followed Bozieka up a narrow creaky staircase to a small room in a gable just under the eaves of the house. There was a window in the gable that framed the town clock, which chimed very loudly for a full minute every hour on the hour. The bed was plump with a fresh puffy white cover filled with goose down and big square pillows.

"Fresh diapers," Bozieka said, pointing to a stack of neatly folded cloths.

"Oh, that is so nice of you. Thank you so much," Reuven said, nodding and even giving a little bit of a bow. The small mouth ripped a few stitches in a slightly bigger smile. "And where, may I ask, is our basket?"

"In the kitchen. I have filled it with food already for tomorrow."

"Oh, thank you. You are too kind."

Again, the small little smile. This time the painted eyebrows seemed to slide toward her hairline. Bozieka wore her dark hair pulled back in a tight bun. Everything about Bozieka was very tight—her hair, her smile, even her skin. Her fingers swelled like sausages in casings, and she had no wrists, just a deep crease where her plump hands met the ends of her arms. As she had led them up the stairs, Reuven had noticed that her ankles puffed up and seemed about to burst over her tightly laced shoes. *Stick her with a pin and she just might pop*, Reuven had thought. It was as if she were too large for her own skin. After she left, he changed Rachel's nappy, poured fresh water in the bowl, and wiped her face and then his own face. Finally they both crawled into bed.

But Rachel did not want to settle down. She squirmed and wriggled. Reuven marveled how with her few little words, she managed to be so demanding. She wanted a drink of water. She wanted a cake.

"No, Rachel, you've had too much already, you'll get a tummy ache," Reuven said.

She scrambled toward the window, which was right by their bed, and began drawing pictures in the frosted glass with her finger.

"It's time for sleep, Rachel, not play."

She began humming, which was her sign that Reuven was supposed to play her a song on his violin.

"No, Rachel, I don't have my violin right now."

"Night night," Rachel said and flopped on the mattress. Two seconds later she popped up again.

"Good morning," her voice rang out cheerfully.

Reuven groaned. It was the Night Night game. Saying "Night night!" a dozen times, she would close her eyes tight and even make a snoring noise for a few seconds, then pop up again and say, "Good morning!" But now when she sat up instead of singing out "Good morning!" she said, "Mama?" The word dropped into the dimness of the attic room. Reuven was silent. "Dada?"

Panic welled in the back of his throat. What was he to do? Oh God, he prayed, what was he to do?

"Time for sleep, Rachel," he said. But Rachel was scrambling out of bed.

Reuven was dead tired. *I might have to spank her*, he thought. Why couldn't this child just get sleepy? Why did she have to be playing games with him after he had schlepped her on his back over thirty miles? How did you deal with a thing like this? How had his mother stood it?

Somehow he managed to lure Rachel back to bed with the promise of a story, her favorite, the froggy story. He tucked her in beside him.

"Once upon a time there was this frog, but he was no ordinary frog." Reuven paused and looked straight into Rachel's eyes and opened his own wide. "And do you know why?"

Rachel made a little sound that sounded a little bit like why.

"Because it was a magic frog," Reuven continued.

By the time he spoke a few more sentences, Rachel was fast asleep.

"Stick your fingers through the bars, children. Let me see how fat you are."

"No, Rachel! No! Don't. It's a trick."

"I want to pet froggy."

"That's not a frog, it's a witch. She wants to roast us in the oven and eat us."

"Not a witch, Reuvie. Pig. See two fat piggies."

Their skin was so tight over their fat you knew they would pop if you pricked them. One with funny black eyebrows.

"Have another tart, children," said the other pig.

"We like them plump," said the pig with the eyebrows.

The pigs were drooling, their eyes gleaming. "Ummm . . . so good with cabbage and a cherry liquor."

"Oh piggies!" squealed Rachel with delight and stuck her finger through the bars.

"No!" shouted Reuven.

Reuven sat bolt upright in bed. He was cold with his own sweat. His heart thumped wildly in his chest. It was a dream, but not just a dream. It was more. He and Rachel had to get out of here now. He knew this as he had never known anything in his life. They must leave quickly. This priest, this house was bad. He was no friend of Jews. There was no time to waste, but how would they get down the creaky stairs without being heard? Reuven glanced out the window. The minute hand on the clock was within a sliver of twelve. The clock would chime for a full minute. They must make their way down the stairs while it was chiming. Their basket was in the kitchen. They had their clothes here, except for their coats and the skirt and the heavy shawl that he had wrapped Rachel in.

Reuven moved quickly. He put on his shoes, pants, and thick boiled wool shirt.

"We must go," he whispered to a sleepy Rachel. He pulled on her dress, stockings, and shoes. He picked her up and grabbed the diapers set out on the bureau. Luckily Rachel was still half asleep. He paused at the top of the stairs. He waited one two three four seconds, and then the clock began to chime. The entire house seemed to reverberate with the din of the clock's ringing.

He was down the steps and across the parlor within the first thirty seconds. He went down the hall into the kitchen. There was his basket by the kitchen stove. His skirt and their heavy outer garments lay in a heap beside it. The pockets on his coat had been turned inside out. The basket was completely empty. None of the promised food packages. It was clear that the basket and his clothes had been searched. For what? Identification papers, money? He slipped the diapers into the basket and then Rachel, who was actually snoring softly. A blessing. He stuffed in the skirt. He had taken it off when they had approached the outskirts of Posva, so when they had appeared at the door, he had looked like an ordinary boy. They probably thought he was using the skirt to wrap up Rachel for warmth. Fine.

A hunk of cold veal sat on a plate with a knife and beside it, a loaf of bread. Too bad he had forgotten the cakes upstairs. But there was a bowl of the sugared nuts by the plate. He emptied them into his pockets. He stuffed the bread in the basket with Rachel, along with the veal, and swung the basket onto his back. Rachel still slept. He spotted some apples in a bowl and was just reaching for them when a scalding voice lashed out at him.

"Whatcha doing?" It was Bozieka. She stood there, voluminous in her white nightgown, her meaty face glowering. Reuven was transfixed. The eyebrows were gone and her features seemed marooned like tiny islands in her huge red face. He saw the small mouth move like the hole in a drawstring purse. There was something both horrifying and fascinating about the face and its features. She was moving toward him. The mouth was opening and shutting. The words were arranging themselves into phrases.

"You can't leave here, boy."

"What do you mean?"

"Father's got the constable coming."

Father? What father? It took Reuven a minute to realize that she meant the priest. She opened her eyes wider and nodded her head, a slight smile creased her face.

"And the patrol too. No, no, you're not going anywhere. Father Groff's got plans for you, Jew boy. And for all of the Jews. We'll be rewarded in heaven for delivering you Christ killers." *And rewarded here,* Reuven thought, remembering the silver platters, the Turkish rugs, the two fat pigs stuffing themselves with food. From the corner of his eye something glinted. He remembered the knife next to the veal. In one swift movement, his hand swiped it off the tabletop. Bozieka didn't seem to even notice. Her small, colorless eyes bore into them.

"You try to stop us and I'll kill you," Reuven said in a low even voice. The knife was at his side. Perhaps she didn't see it.

"Phutt." She spat at him and continued to advance. "You're a Jew boy. We can kill you. God protects us."

She must not be seeing the knife, he thought. Should he threaten her? She was less than an arm's length away.

He never knew exactly how it happened, although he remembered thinking was that threats were a waste of time. Had he made a move toward her? Had he raised the knife? But the next thing he knew, she was standing in front of him bleeding. A red blossom had begun to spread on her nightgown as blood poured from the thin slit in her hand. They both stood there in a stunned silence, each disbelieving what had just occurred. A voice battered somewhere in the back of Reuven's brain. *MOVE!*

He flew out the door. When he passed the clock, he looked up. It was three minutes after midnight. Three minutes. It felt like a lifetime. He ran out of the west end of the town. There was a post with signs to Grodno, Vilna, Bielsk, Slonim, and Bransk. He turned right, to the north, and followed the sign that pointed to Vilna.

ELEVEN

REUVEN HAD gone several kilometers down the road toward Vilna before he realized that he still had the knife in his hand. It was smeared with the horrid woman's blood. He stopped as an appalling thought struck him. Suppose this knife had dripped her blood. A trail of blood! What if they sent bloodhounds after him? He looked down. There didn't seem to be any drops of blood on his pants or coat or on the road. Still, he decided he should get rid of it. He had just raised his hand to heave it into a ditch when he thought better of it. This was the only weapon he had. Perhaps he should not be so quick to throw it away. And it was more than just a weapon, it could also be a useful tool. Reuven walked to a bank of snow by the side of the road. He wiped the knife in the snow until the smear of blood was completely gone.

Rachel had begun to stir on his back. He hoped she would sleep some more, but she had slept when it really counted so he shouldn't complain now.

He planned to walk as far as he could on this road until the first light of the new day broke. Then he would take to the woods. It was a good road with lots of trees and shrubs to hide them, and he wanted to stay with it as long as he could.

He figured with the long nights and the short days of this month of December, he had at least six or seven more hours of walking time in the shadows of the night and into the gray light of the dawn. Then he would need to rest. He would be dead tired. Barns were very tempting to sleep in, but there was the danger of the farmer coming out and discovering you. There was someplace, or the memory of a place, that seemed to nag at the back of his mind. A taste swam up in his mouth—the taste of those sour apples. Then it burst upon him—that place near Berischeva! When he had stuck his hands down into the snowy hollows formed by the drifts around the apple trees' roots and found those apples that even the worms had deserted. But he remembered being surprised how comparatively warm the air felt within those hollows. Even the apples themselves were somewhat warm when by all rights they should have been frozen solid.

Of course not! He remembered a book of Uncle Chizor's with the engravings of the Eskimo people in their snow huts. Uncle Chizor had explained to him that snow can act as insulation. The packed snow blocks out the wind. The spaces between the snowflake crystals trap air.

When dawn came, he found a deep drift. He tunneled out a little snow cave for himself and Rachel. The knife was helpful, although his little snow cave hardly looked like the neat igloos he had seen in the pictures in his uncle's book. But it kept Rachel and him fairly warm. A wind had come up during the night that would have been bitter if they had been exposed. Reuven liked the snow cave. It was cozy and bright and most important, he felt safe. He and Rachel were hidden away as completely as animals in their winter hibernation. Unfortunately, they were not hibernating, so they could not stay in the snow cave forever. As soon as the darkness fell, they had to be off. Vilna, he figured, could not be more than thirty kilometers away. They should be able to make it easily within two or three days at the most.

The next day an extraordinary thing happened. Rachel had been whimpering. The whimpering always started in a vague, sporadic way. She would not immediately call for her mama, but with dread Reuven could almost see her lips begin to press together to make a wretched little humming noise, like a prelude to the sound "mmmm" and finally the word "mama" would tear from her. But this time the "mmm" sound was cut short and then he heard her squeal, "Chickie! Chickie!"

Straight ahead in the road was a chicken that had seemingly appeared out of thin air. There were no farms nearby, and Reuven guessed that a cart must have passed this way and a chicken had escaped from its coop without the driver noticing. Chickens were not to be passed up. And this one seemed a bit weary from his time on the road. Indeed it seemed so pleased to see another living thing that when Reuven bent down to grab it, the bird practically flew into his arms. He ran to the side of the road. Pressing it down on a rock, he chopped off its head with the knife.

"Uh-oh!" said Rachel as the head fell into the snow.

That night the sky was clear, and with the moon nearly full, there would not be much camouflage on the road. Reuven felt that it might be best to stay in the woods while traveling. They were so tired they stopped early and Reuven built a small fire. He had plucked the chicken and chopped it into roasting-size pieces. Rachel had played with the feathers while he had prepared their dinner. He should have brought those cakes from the priest's house. A sweet would have tasted good. They had a bit of bread with the chicken.

"We are eating well, Miss Rachel, considering," he said as he handed her a piece of chicken.

"Considering." Rachel said the word clearly.

Reuven looked at her in amazement. How quickly she was learning.

Reuven wondered how much he could teach her. "Drumstick," he said, pointing at the piece of chicken she was eating.

"No, chicken," she replied fiercely.

"Well, yes it is a chicken, but that part of the chicken leg is called a drumstick."

"No, chicken," she said.

"Okay, chicken."

"Okay, chicken," she repeated

This baby was a wonder. He would try and teach her the latke rhyme.

"I have a little potato.
It's nice and round.
I'm going to chop it up
and fry it golden brown.
It's a little latke
ready to go
right into my potke
and I want more!"

"Again!" Rachel demanded. He said it once more, then twice more. After five times, Reuven was bored silly. "Come on, Rachel, you have to say it too."

"Mama," Rachel said. The game suddenly stopped.

"Mama? No, Rachel." His face turned stern. "We're singing the latke song."

"Mama," Rachel repeated. "Mama, Papa, Prinka."

The trees around them swirled. The flames of their small fire suddenly became tongues, all crying "Mama." Rachel's face had turned red, her cheeks slick with tears. Reuven felt a panic seize him. What should he do? He reached for Rachel and grabbed her to him, pressing her to his chest. He buried his face in the thick nubbly knit of her little wool hat. He could smell her hair through it. He could smell her diaper. What in God's name was he to do with this smelly howling baby in the middle of Russia?

"This isn't fair!" he cried. "This is not fair! I can't be doing this. I know nothing about babies. I am not a father. I am not a mother. I am a brother. They are gone, Rachel! They are gone! They are all gone!"

"Gone," Rachel said. The single word rang like a chime in the dense forest. She looked up and touched his wet cheeks. He saw a look of confusion in her eyes. She scrambled out of his lap and stood up.

"Gone." She said the word again and paused, as if she were listening to its sound. "Gone, gone, gone." She stomped her feet on the cleared ground near their fire. It was a sound to her, a meaningless sound. In that instant, Reuven realized that fairness had nothing to do with anything. They had each other, and that was all they had in this world. It was all that counted.

As Rachel stomped on the ground and repeated the word, he watched her antic shadow lace between the light of the flames cast from the fire, her little arms jerking, her head bobbing. Her shadow grew longer until it became tangled with his own shadow's hunched still form. The little shadow stomped away and stretched. With the little peaked cap, it could have been that of a fierce devil of the woods—the arms slashing the night frantically in some kind of manic dance.

"Gone! Gone! Gone!" Rachel's voice roared into the blackness of the night.

TWELVE

60 KILOMETERS TO VILNA.

"No! It can't be." Reuven stared at the sign at the crossroads dumbfounded. They had been on the road for three days already. He had been sure they would be in Vilna tonight. He thought he had already crossed the Russian-Polish border. But he had been mistaken. This sign meant three more days, three more days at least! He was exhausted. They had eaten the last of the veal. His left foot had a blister the size of a latke. They were out of clean nappies, and Rachel stunk to high heaven.

Suddenly he heard rowdy voices. From the other road that led at a right angle into the main road where they now stood, Reuven saw a group of men. Not just any men. They were Cossacks, and not just any Cossacks. By the light of the now full moon Reuven could see the flash of the gold braid, the white plumes on their helmets, and the silver glint of their crossed bandoliers. They were the most elite contingent, part of the tsar's personal regiment.

"Oy yoy yoy!" Reuven gasped.

"Oy yoy yoy." Rachel mimicked him perfectly.

Reuven immediately dropped to his knees with Rachel still in her basket strapped to his back. They had to get as low to the ground as possible. The side of the road dipped into a deep culvert. He scrambled for it. The snow had melted, and he felt the wet marshy ground beneath his knees. Luckily there was a screen of thick weeds and stalks, now sere and dry, from the previous summer. He slipped the basket from his shoulders and pulled Rachel out. He felt better holding her in his arms. If she began to talk too loudly, he could put his hand over her mouth.

"Hungry," she demanded. He reached for their last hunk of bread and gave it to her.

He put his finger to his mouth. "Ssshh. You must be very quiet, Rachel."

She put her finger up to her mouth and very loudly said, "Ssssh."

"No, Rachel. I mean it—very quiet."

They could now hear the thud of the horses' hooves. There was drunken singing. Maybe the soldiers were too drunk to notice them. But if they were discovered, drunk Cossacks were the worst of all. The alcohol made them terrible. The clouds scudded off the moon and the entire landscape turned silvery bright. It was a warm night for this time of year, and there was a dampness in the air. Reuven watched as a fringe of tiny beads of moisture collected on Rachel's dark eyelashes, turning them silver. Then a long shadow cut across the drainage ditch and against the bleached ground—a horse's head snorting and tossing that appeared like a moving silhouette. Then there was a crisscross of shadows as dozens of horses' legs latticed the night. It was as if he and Rachel were being trampled by shadows. The Cossacks were so close. Reuven could have almost reached up and touched one of the clopping hooves. The tall black boots in silver stirrups glimmered with the light of the moon.

A tiny voice began to sing. "I have a little potato—"

Reuven clapped his hand over Rachel's mouth. She squirmed violently in his arms. He felt her hot little breath trying to scream. Why in God's name did she have to choose this time to sing the latke song? Her feet were thrashing now. His other arm wrapped around her legs. He looked in her face. Never had he seen such fury in her eyes. *She is hating me, but by God this is the way it has to be!* he vowed.

Reuven did not know how long it took the Cossacks to pass. It seemed like forever, but it might not have been more than three minutes, as there were only twenty or twenty-five of them. When they finally did pass and he took his hand away from Rachel's face, he did not hear the yowl he had expected. She merely whimpered and rubbed her nose. This made him feel worse.

"I'm sorry, Rachel. I really am." She didn't even look up at him.

Although the Cossacks had headed off in the opposite direction from Vilna, Reuven made a quick decision that the moonlight was too bright for them to be out on this road. It was a good road too, and with still sixty kilometers to go he was reluctant to leave it for the shelter of the thick forest. Perhaps tomorrow the night would be cloudy and they could travel on it again. But for now the safer choice was to go into the woods. So with Rachel on his back, he climbed out of the ditch and headed across a barren field to the wooded land at its far edge.

There was much less snow in these woods than the others they had been in, and he heard the howl of what could only be a wolf. But what was a wild wolf next to a Cossack? The thought caught him up short. Children were supposed to be afraid of wolves. There were dozens of stories about wolves slipping into pastures and killing sheep or worse, sliding through the shadows of the night right into homes where they would snatch babies from their cradles. But he could not imagine that wolves could be any more savage than the Cossacks who had broken into their home in Berischeva and murdered his parents and sister. Wolves might even be reasonable in comparison. So the occasional howl that laced the night air did not disturb Reuven as it would have two weeks before.

Suddenly the trees in the forest seemed to thin and he found himself in a clearing.

"What's this?" he asked. But there was no "uh-oh" popping up from the basket, only the soft snoring sounds of Rachel, who was sound asleep. Reuven squinted. There was this clearing and then a short way beyond it, no more than one hundred meters away, he could swear he spied another road. He began walking quickly.

Indeed it was a road, and not a bad one at that. He had no idea which way to turn on it, left or right. But he saw a sign post to the left so he began walking toward it. There was only one marker pointing west. The words were BRYZNCK 2 KILOMETERS. He read the name and then said it again out loud. Where had he heard that name before? Like a bell with a muffled clapper, the name rang dimly somewhere in his memory.

"Bryznck!" he burst out.

"Uh-oh." Rachel raised her head, fully alert now.

"Bryznck! Rachel, Bryznck!" Of course, Bryznck was the village of the Baron Radzinsky, Uncle Chizor's baron! And it was only two kilometers away. Reuven must have crossed the border into Poland without even knowing it. He knew that the baron's house was very near the border. Vilna was still sixty kilometers north, according to the sign on the road where he had encountered the Cossacks. The only thing he could figure was that somehow he had gained distance west toward Poland but was much farther south than he had anticipated. He didn't know. He didn't care. His only thought was to get to the baron's estate. It would not be hard. He remembered from his uncle's descriptions that there was barely a town. Whatever townspeople did exist worked primarily on the estates of the baron, who owned virtually all the surrounding land. The road took a sharp swing to the right. A sign appeared, announcing in both Russian and Polish that at this point the lands of the baron Drago Radzinsky began and all hunting was expressly forbidden.

"Come on, Rachel. Let's go."

The big iron gates leading into the baron's estate were shut. But it did not take Reuven more than five minutes to find a way in by scrambling over the stone pilings that anchored each end of the gates. And now he was on the drive. It was just like Uncle Chizor had described. Huge white oaks on either side of the drive. When he looked to the east, he could see a faint rose tint in the sky as the skin of the night peeled away and the first light of the new day broke. He supposed that he and Rachel should not knock on the door as soon as they got there. It would be awfully early. He imagined that barons slept late. In the distance he could just make out the portico. In another five minutes, they would be there.

He saw the lions, and then suddenly their stone mouths seemed to drop open and out rushed the most bloodcurdling barks. Reuven felt Rachel lurch in her basket and scream. Five hounds with their fangs bared raced around the corner of the portico and lunged at them. He did not run. Instead, some instinct made him drop to his knees. Keeping his eyes down, he extended his open palms to the dogs. He crooned softly the melody of one of the first Chopin etudes he had ever learned on the violin. The dogs' barks became a blend of whelpings and mewlings and they began to back away. A shadow in the pink light of morning moved over him.

"A baby?" a man said first in Polish and then quickly in Russian. Reuven felt a hand cup his chin.

"Up, my boy," the man said.

Reuven raised himself up, still shaking from the dogs. He did not have to ask. He knew that the man standing before him with the neatly trimmed salt-and-pepper beard, the patch over one eye, and the scar that sliced diagonally down the left cheek was Baron Drago Radzinsky.

"Sir, my name is Reuven Bloom and this is my sister, Rachel. Our uncle is Chizor Bloom. Chizor has gone to

America already, but our village was burned. Our mother and father and sister were killed by the Cossacks. Rachel and I are all that is left."

Reuven dared now to look directly into the baron's face. He saw that the man had become very pale. His eyes were filled with a dim sad light and his mouth quivered.

"So these dogs were nothing next to the Cossacks. I understand." He spoke in such a low voice that Reuven almost had to strain to hear him.

THIRTEEN

"THEY TOOK your violin?"

"He took it—one man, a Cossack."

Reuven was sitting at the baron's table. Despite the richness of the furnishings, Baron Radzinsky's table was simply laid. There were not the piles of food that had been set out on the priest's table, and nobody was trying to stuff Reuven and Rachel. In deference to the children's coming from a kosher household, which forbade the serving of meat and dairy in the same meal, the baron had announced they would have a dairy meal.

"The baby needs milk, no doubt," he had said.

They had eggs and cheese and milk and a thick vegetable soup. It tasted wonderful. There were some chocolate biscuits for dessert, no rich cream cakes with jewel-like decorations as in the priest's house.

"So one man took away your dear Ceruti. How I looked for that for you. What the hell is a Cossack going to do with a violin like that?" The unspoken question hung in the air. How could someone who had just murdered a young girl play a beautiful instrument crafted by a family that had adored fine music for generations? Could a murderer play Brahms?

Suddenly a flood of images rushed into Reuven's mind. He had tried so hard not to think about that day. He had tried to block the images of the blood from his sister's throat, the crumpled bodies of his parents that lay outside their front door. But those horrible pictures were never far beneath the surface of his conscience. Another image now loomed up in his mind's eye. It was the face of the Cossack. He had never realized until this moment that he had registered every feature, every small aspect of that face. The man had pale red hair. His face was pockmarked and there was a large pit in the side of his nose. His eyebrows were a much darker red than the color of his beard and the hair on his head. His brow protruded, and with the dark red eyebrows, it cast his eyes into a deep shadow. The eyes, a light icy blue, seemed to shine out from the shadow like two cold stars. Yes, Reuven remembered that face and would until the day he died.

"Reuven! Reuven!" The baron was speaking to him sharply and shaking his shoulder. "Are you all right, Reuven?"

Rachel was whimpering.

"Oh!" Reuven said softly. He felt as if he were being

called back from a distant place. He suddenly realized that his cheeks were wet. He must have been crying.

"You are very tired, Reuven," the baron said. "I'll show you to your room."

The room was a large one with a fireplace in which three logs crackled. A young servant girl helped undress and bathe Rachel in a dressing room with a large porcelain tub. Fresh hot water was brought for Reuven. When he was finished and had tucked himself into bed, and Rachel into the small one that had been brought in for her, he heard a soft knock on the door.

"Come in," Reuven said.

The baron peeked his head in the door. "I am only here to say good night. We can talk tomorrow."

But now Reuven felt oddly untired.

"No, it is fine." He paused. "I think I want to talk." Rachel was almost asleep. The baron walked over and sat on the edge of Reuven's bed. His shoulders sagged and he shook his head in a despairing manner.

"Well, I am glad that Chizor is alive somewhere, but I shudder when I think what you have experienced, my boy."

"Before we ate when we were sitting in your library, I saw so many beautiful books. Some were Shakespeare."

"You know about Shakespeare?"

"Oh yes. Uncle Chizor had many Shakespeare plays and he taught me and my sister to love him, and all the fairy-tale writers as well. He told us that you found most of these books for him."

"Well, not exactly. Many, yes. But Chizor had a cousin or someone in Vilna who is a book dealer."

"Sperling! Lovotz Sperling."

"That's the one."

"How could I have forgotten he was a book dealer! He is the man I am supposed to go to."

"Yes, yes. He deals mostly in old Jewish books, but he gets a few other things as well. There is more demand for Shakespeare now among the Jews."

"Why is that, and why had I never heard Uncle Chizor or my father speak of this man before?"

"Actually, the answer to both your questions is strangely enough almost the same. The Jews, especially the Jews around Vilna, are no longer reading just Talmud."

"They aren't?"

"No, they are reading some Shakespeare and a lot of Marx."

"Marx? Is he a playwright too?"

"No, hardly—or perhaps." The baron paused, scratched his chin, and looked up at the ceiling in the bedroom. "Yes, perhaps he has some kind of a play in mind. Let me tell you." Reuven was not sure if he was following this conversation. "Marx envisions a new world order where workers control the means of production and are paid according to their needs. A classless society. No aristocracy. No tsars, and"—a dim smile crossed his face—"no barons." He shrugged. "But the important thing now is not just what the Vilna Jews are reading, but what they are doing. They have organized themselves into a league for political activity. And this league is called the Bund."

Reuven propped himself up onto his elbow. "The Bund? What does it stand for? What do they do?"

"The full name is the Algemayner Yidisher Arbayter of Lithuania, Poland, and Russia—the Jewish Workers' Federation. It is a social democratic movement. They have recently started a newspaper. They want workers to unite. They want to call strikes and boycotts to correct unfair working conditions. They want fair wages and better treatment for every worker, Jew or non-Jew. They want a modern world brought to Russia and Poland."

"A modern world?" whispered Reuven. What did he know about a modern world? He had spent nearly his entire life in a little tiny Jewish shtetl in the Pale. It was only because of his Uncle Chizor that he knew of Shakespeare. It was only because his parents had believed in his talent as a musician that he played a violin and the old masters' music. But what did he really know of the modern world?

What the baron was saying, however, was so exciting he almost dared not think about it too much. These people, these members of the Bund were trying to make Russia a world in which everyone could live—Jew or non-Jew. If they could succeed—well it was too late for his mother and father and Shriprinka, but think of all the other mothers and fathers, all the other Shriprinkas who were still alive in little shtetls. . . . Were they just waiting to be killed?

"They are revolutionaries," the baron said in a low voice.

"Revolutionaries!" The very air in the room seemed

to quiver with the word. "And the second part of the question?" Reuven remembered suddenly.

"Ah yes, why you never heard your uncle or father speak of Lovotz Sperling."

"Yes." Reuven nodded. "Why?"

"Your cousin Sperling is the very center of the Bund. It was on his little alley, in the attic of his shop, where the first meeting took place in Vilna. It was there that the original members of the Bund—representatives from cities all over Poland and Russia, from Vilna, Bialystok, Minsk, Kovno, Vitebsk, Moscow, and Warsaw—first gathered."

"My cousin?"

"Yes, your cousin. It is a dangerous position to be in—that is probably why your uncle and father never mentioned him. I knew of him because of your uncle, and of course my interest in collecting books had led me to him some years back, even before I had become close with Chizor."

"But you say he is dangerous. Is this where Rachel and I should be going?"

"There is no safe place for any Jew now. Lovotz will know how to take care of you. He shall know what to do."

"He is a revolutionary, then."

"He is the Firebrand! That is his nickname in Yiddish, *bren*."

FOURTEEN

"'IF I am not for myself, who will be for me? But if I am only for myself, what am I? And if not now, when?'" This was a firebrand. Yes, the words that came from his mouth were as fiery and bright as little licks of flame, but Lovotz Sperling was not what Reuven had imagined. He was a little wisp of a man, at least a head shorter than Reuven. His dark eyes were obscured behind spectacles with the thickest lenses Reuven had ever seen. He had a withered left arm that had grown not much bigger than a baby's and hung limply by his side. And now he was reciting the motto of the Bund to Reuven.

"It is not all that original. It comes from Hillel, a Jewish sage. We adopted it. It describes our philosophy perfectly." His wife, Basia, a large woman, beamed as her husband spoke.

Reuven and Rachel had arrived on the little alley off Szeroka Street three days before, delivered in the baron's coach. Lovotz and Basia welcomed them. They had already heard of the terrible massacre in Berischeva and they were completely stunned that anyone, let alone relatives of theirs, had survived. They both wept. They wept as if they had known Rachel and Reuven all their lives.

Lovotz and Basia had three very young children, one

just slightly older than Rachel. They were all fascinated by the new arrivals in their home. One by one the children came out with a toy or a biscuit or a piece of dried fruit and offered it to Rachel. Then the oldest child, a girl of about eight called Miri, took Rachel by the hand.

"Do you want to see our house for dollies?" she asked.

"No. I want to show her the secret place," said her brother Yossel, who was about four.

Soon Rachel was playing with them—looking at their dolls, spinning their tops, sitting at a child-size table being served pretend tea. It was not until the next day that Lovotz sat down and explained about the Bund to Reuven.

"So you see," Lovotz said, "we are all interlocked, like this." With difficulty he raised his withered arm and laced his fingers together, turning them inward toward his palms, so that only the knuckles showed. "It does not matter that I am a bookseller and that Shlomo is a cobbler or Yakov is a knitter. Our struggles are the same, and through sharing our struggles, we gain strength. You say well, as a book dealer, I am not a tradesman. And the cobbler and the knitters and the glove makers are merely tradesmen. There is no 'merely' with a revolution. Everything and everyone counts.

"We go full steam, full blast for one another no matter who we are as individuals. In that way, we succeed. Three years ago the weavers had a strike, and it was a victory. We are now extending and coordinating our strike activities. We are planning strategies with our trade unions. And believe me, this is the way to revolution and the way to end all the suffering of the enslaved. You see, we print these." He took a leaflet out of his pocket. There was a picture of the tsar drawn on the front and the words: *Prepare for the coming bloody struggle with despotism. End the suffering of the weak, the enslaved, the exploited.* Reuven could feel Lovotz watching him as he read the pamphlet.

"We print them—right here, as a matter of fact. But we have many supporters from all over. We get money and even paper for printing from America. The Jewish people in America are as excited about our Bund as the people here in Russia and Poland. We get lots of support. And that is why Basia and the children are going soon to America."

"What? They are going to America?"

"Yes, and we must talk about this. Basia is our best fund-raiser. She speaks Russian and Polish and Lithuanian and has even been learning English." Reuven had sensed that Basia was different from most traditional Jewish wives. She participated more in conversations. He rarely saw her without a book in one hand, even when she was stirring a pot on the stove or feeding a child.

"It is getting too dangerous now for Basia and the children." Lovotz paused. "I do not need to tell you how dangerous it is getting. And it will get worse before it gets better, before the revolution." He stopped again. When he spoke again he did not look directly at Reuven. "The baron Radzinsky is a truly noble man. He is an aristocrat not simply of birth but of spirit. He has given me enough money for both you and your sister's passage to America."

Reuven could hardly believe his ears. "I can't believe

it! This is too wonderful." He gasped. He was to go to the *Goldeneh Medina.* He would find Uncle Chizor. He and Rachel would get out of the *farshtinkener* country forever. To America! Rachel toddled into the room. He swept her up.

"Rachel, we are going to America. Can you believe it? Rachel, you and me in America!" And he pictured the strangely shaped blue claw of lakes on his uncle's map and then the place called Florida that hung like a sausage into the ocean and far to the west, California and the Pacific Ocean. He pictured it all—a vast continent in which there was no Pale and where Jews could live anyplace they chose. Rachel wriggled out of his arms and began dancing a little jig.

"America America!" she cried.

But he knew that she no more understood the meaning of the word *America* than she had the word *gone* she had chanted when they were on the road. Still the din of her high voice and the stomp of her feet made a pleasant melody in Reuven's ears.

But suddenly within this din, between the cries of "America" and the stomp of Rachel's little feet, Reuven sensed a pocket of silence. Lovotz Sperling was sitting perfectly still, simply staring at his hand, which rested on the table. Was there something wrong?

Reuven reached out for Rachel and told her to hush.

"Is there something wrong, Lovotz? Did the baron really give you the money or are you having to pay for us?"

"Oh no no, my boy." He looked up and shook his head, but there was a trace of sadness in his eyes.

They would be leaving for America in a week. They would take a train to Austria, then another to Germany, and then board a ship in Bremen. Basia was sewing like crazy. She made new dresses and warm little caps for Rachel and new trousers for Reuven. The family's generosity knew no bounds.

Lovotz escorted Reuven all over Vilna. He took him to the cafés where he met the head of the cobblers' and the weavers' unions. He took him to the *shulhoyf*, the courtyard of the great synagogue where the gifted scholar, the Vilna Gaon, Elijah Ben Solomon Zalman, had held forth a century before. They wound their way through the labyrinth of alleys and covered passageways of the Jewish quarter. In Berischeva, it seemed that all the shops had to do with the physical necessities of life—markets, locksmiths, carpenters, cobblers. But here in Vilna there was all that and more. There were bookshops, chess clubs, a writers' café, and yes, even a music store that sold instruments and sheet music! They stopped now in front of one on the daily walk that had become part of Reuven and Lovotz's routine.

"Go on in, Reuven. We have passed at least three shops like this in the last two days and I always see you slow down then quickly hurry along. You have lost your violin, my boy, but you haven't lost your music. Go in."

"But I can't afford anything."

"Of course you can't. You're going to America. You hardly have money to spare."

"I have no money at all." Reuven laughed.

"But you can still look."

✦ ✦ ✦

Reuven and Lovotz walked into the store. The owner greeted Lovotz warmly.

"Shalom, Isaac."

"Shalom, dear Lovotz." The shopkeeper came up and embraced him. "How goes it all?" *So even music store owners are part of the Bund*, Reuven thought to himself.

"Meet my cousin Reuven. A violinist—a gifted one, I believe."

Isaac was a tall gaunt man with wiry hair and very dark eyes. His sharp nose pointed down at such a steep angle it seemed in danger of sliding off his face. He raised one eyebrow and began to speak.

"Aah, we have many good violinists here in Vilna. You know, the academy and all. We turn out some very fine violinists."

"Turn out" seemed an odd way to talk about music or any kind of art or artist. But maybe this was part of this new industrial way of speaking. Reuven had heard much of this in the last few days. Basia and Lovotz were constantly talking about production, labor, and market value. But could you talk about art in this way? It wasn't piecework. It wasn't a product.

Isaac had disappeared behind a tall counter. When he came out in front, he held a beautiful violin.

"A Guarneri," he said.

"A Guarneri!" Reuven exclaimed.

"Aah, he knows a Guarneri!" Isaac spoke in a slightly patronizing tone.

"Of course!" Reuven said.

"Try it," Isaac said.

"All right."

Instinctively Reuven tuned the instrument and began to play the Dvořák, the piece that Uncle Chizor had brought the night of the seder. He remembered to stress the first six notes and then follow with great calmness on the next measures. Within seconds he was lost in the music. He had never heard such a sound come from a violin. It was right what they said about the Guarneris. There was a purity of sound that was unbelievable. So pure yet so warm.

When he had finished playing, Isaac came out from behind the counter. He put his hand gently on Reuven's head. There were tears in his yes. "You're the finest I have ever heard," he said simply. Then he turned Lovotz. "Take him to the academy. They must hear him there."

"It will only frustrate them."

"Lovotz, what are you talking about?"

"The boy leaves for America in two days."

"Aah, I see." Isaac shook his head.

And once more Reuven spied that faint shadow in his cousin Lovotz's eyes. Was it that Lovotz was sad for him to be going to America because he wanted him to continue his music studies here? But Lovotz had said it was becoming too dangerous. If it was too dangerous for his wife and children, was it not too dangerous for him and Rachel? Reuven was confused. As they left the shop and walked down the street, both Reuven and his cousin fell into an uncomfortable silence. There were things that Reuven wanted to ask, but he was afraid to, and he felt that there might be things his cousin wanted to say but that he also was hesitant.

"Let's stop here and get a coffee," said Lovotz.

It was the writers' café. They had been there once before. Reuven had noticed that there were a lot of women similar to Basia at the tables—intense, with their noses stuck in books or often arguing loudly with the men. They dressed immodestly too. His own mother had never appeared without a kerchief or wearing her Jewish wig, her *sheitel.* These women, well perhaps they were not married, but they exposed their own hair, and many of them wore dresses with open collars and sleeves that did not reach the wrists. They were full of talk and humor, and the men were often the butt of their jokes.

Lovotz ordered coffee for them both.

"Different from Berischeva, eh?" he asked.

"Yes!" Reuven took a deep breath. The words just came to him. "Cousin, it is as if you just read my mind. Are you a mind reader?"

"Not quite, and I doubt that I read all of your thoughts."

"No." Reuven paused. "I wish you could."

"How do you mean, Reuven?"

"Cousin Lovotz, something is bothering you. I know that."

"Now *who* is the mind reader?" Lovotz sighed and muttered to himself.

"What?"

"Basia would be furious."

"What are you talking about?"

Lovotz looked directly into Reuven's eyes. "Reuven, this is very difficult. You are right. Something is troubling me, and in truth I have no right to be troubled by this."

Reuven waited, not saying a word.

"I . . ." Reuven could tell that Lovotz was searching for the right words. "I was hoping, Reuven dear boy, I was hoping that you might want to . . ." He was speaking very slowly now, as if weighing every word. "Become a member of the Bund and that instead of going to America, you might remain here with us and . . . and . . ."

"Join the revolution." Reuven finished the sentence.

"Yes." Lovotz looked down at his hand on the table. His pale cheeks flushed slightly.

"But what about Rachel? I am her brother."

"Right." Lovotz spoke the word emphatically. "You are her brother." Was there an emphasis on the word *her*? Was something left unsaid—that you are *our* brother too?

Lovotz now leaned forward. He heaved up his withered arm, and with both his hands, one shrunken and white the other large and incredibly powerful, he grasped Reuven's hand. It was a very odd sensation. One of Lovotz's hands felt limp and even cold, the other was warm and seemed to tingle with life.

"Look . . ." Then Lovotz's eyes rolled toward heaven. "God forgive me. Look . . ." He began again. "We need you. You are young and strong. You speak Russian well. You are smart and quick. You would be invaluable."

"But Rachel?"

"Rachel is a baby."

Please, prayed Reuven, *don't say she is so young she will forget me. Please don't say that.*

"But already you see how she loves our children. Basia will take her to America, to New York. We have been sending money to friends there. Basia will take care of her as if she is her own. She will be happy. She will be with other children. She will be in America. In America, she will go to school. She will have a chance. There is no chance here for a Jewish girl. These women who sit here in the café"—he gestured toward the intense women that Reuven had noticed when he came in—"they have fought and fought to get what they have. In most cases, their families hate them for this independence. They have gone against an old and outdated tradition. Yes, they are independent, but they will never be free—not in the way they would be in America. Rachel will remember you. Basia will make sure of that, and someday, probably not so far off, you will go to America too."

Reuven was silent for a long time. What Lovotz Sperling had proposed was unthinkable, unimaginable. He and Rachel had been closer than any two people for these last weeks. He had carried her on his back across the Pale of Russia into Poland. They had hidden in ditches, built snow caves to sleep in. He had cajoled her, scolded her, hushed her, clamped his hand over her screaming mouth, felt the furious light of her dark eyes. She was as much a part of him as a vital organ in his body. To leave her would be like cutting out a part of himself. Why couldn't Lovotz understand any of this? But still, Reuven felt very deeply for his cousin. He felt he owed him a considered opinion. His mouth began to move mechanically. With the first words he knew he was lying, and he knew Lovotz knew it. "I shall think about it, cousin. I shall consider this most carefully. Yes. Lovotz, give me some time. I must get used to the idea. Give me some time."

Lovotz patted his hand. Reuven felt no warmth this

time. It was merely a gesture. "Yes, of course, of course. Shall we go? I think it is time for us to get back home," Lovotz said.

"Yes, cousin."

They got up to leave. As they were walking out of the café, Reuven felt Lovotz pat his shoulder and then grip it with that amazingly strong hand. It was not an empty gesture. It was one full of deep affection. *This man is so good*, Reuven thought.

They were walking by the Strashun Library.

"I will take you there tomorrow. No time today. There are tens of thousands of volumes of ancient Hebrew texts alone. Some are among the earliest ever printed. Yes, indeed, just twenty years after Gutenberg invented the printing press. As a book dealer I am often called in to advise them on the authenticity of certain materials."

They had just turned a corner when something rushed out of an alley. Reuven heard a funny popping noise and was about to turn to Lovotz and ask him what it could be when he suddenly realized that Lovotz was standing stock still and clutching his stomach with a look of frozen horror on his face. Then his cousin crumpled against him. There was almost no weight to the man. A terrible shriek cut the air as both Reuven and Lovotz fell to the cobblestones.

"Cousin!" Reuven gasped as he held Lovotz in his arms. Reuven's right arm, his bow arm, supported the light weight, and he stared in disbelief as he watched his hand turn red with blood. People were rushing up to them.

"My God, it's Lovotz Sperling. . . ."

"The bastards shot Lovotz!"

"Make way . . . give him air."

Reuven thought, *This cannot be happening. Not again. This is not Berischeva.* Scores of people now crowded about them. Reuven looked into Lovotz's face. His eyes were open and focusing on Reuven. A small bubble of blood burbled at the corner of his mouth. He was trying to talk.

"Don't talk, cousin, don't talk. We'll get you to a doctor. Save your strength. Don't talk." *Oh please God,* Reuven prayed, *do not take this good man.*

Lovotz's mouth kept trying to make the words. There was so much blood. So much blood from such a tiny man. Then someone was peeling Reuven off of Lovotz's blood-slicked cloak.

"No no!" Reuven heard himself saying. "I'll stay here with my cousin and help get him to the doctor. He's so light. I am very strong."

He felt someone's touch on his head. "Reuven, he is gone. It is no use."

"No, he is all right, I tell you. Lovotz?"

An arm clasped him. He looked around. It was Isaac, the music shop owner. Tears were streaming down his face.

"They got him." Jagged words tore from Isaac's throat.

What was this man saying? They? Who was they? Why did they want to shoot Lovotz? "I don't understand."

"Agents, my boy. Secret agents. They know about the

Bund. They know how powerful it is becoming." While they talked, Isaac had been moving Reuven away from Lovotz.

"This cannot be." Reuven kept shaking his head and repeating the words.

"It is difficult for the young. You have seen so little." At this Reuven stopped walking. Anger flushed through him. "No, sir, you are mistaken. I have seen too much." And a torrential sob ripped from his throat.

After Lovotz was murdered, it seemed to Reuven that he existed in a timeless zone—unlike when his own family was killed and there had been no time to think but only to act, to snatch Rachel up and run. Now there was time to think. He wondered how in such a short space of time this man Lovotz Sperling had come to occupy such an enormous place in his mind, and then gently invade his heart. He thought back to that afternoon in the writers' café when Lovotz had asked him to become a member of the Bund, to let Basia take Rachel to America. It had been unthinkable then, and even when he had replied that Lovotz should give him some time so he could get used to the idea, Reuven had believed in his heart that he would not consider. But now he had to think about it. He was cornered. Cornered by murder, by blood, and by the shining promise of real safety for Rachel in America—the *Goldeneh Medina*, the Golden Country that had drawn his uncle. Uncle Chizor's words came back to him now. *"But you see, Reuven, I am not a revolutionary. I am a tailor. I have nobody to save except myself.*

I have anger. But I guess not enough to stay and turn the whole place upside down. And I have no patience. Yes, I am an impatient man. Very impatient, and that is why I choose to leave."

But did Reuven have enough anger? Or maybe it was really a question of love. Did he have enough love to let Rachel go?

For Rachel it was a game. It was just like the good night game except it was the good-bye game. She was bundled into her new coat and her new shoes. Basia and the four children stood on the platform where they would catch the train that would take them to Vienna. There they would then catch another train to Bremen, where they would board a ship to America.

"Bye-bye." She kept waving. "Bye-bye, Reuvie." And then she would rush into his arms. What would happen when they all boarded the train and Rachel figured out that her brother wasn't coming? When would this knowledge dawn on her? Reuven and Basia had discussed the departure endlessly. Reuven had thought that he should not come to the train station at all, or perhaps put them all on the train and then quickly disappear before the train pulled out. But Basia was against this.

"No," she had said. "Rachel must see you waving good-bye on the platform. I do not believe in tricking children. She will cry, yes, but we will explain to her that you will be coming to America later on. In the meantime, you will write her letters and send her little presents."

In the end, Reuven had agreed.

◆ ◆ ◆

And now the train was pulling into the station. A porter had been hired to help them with their bags. Basia had it all planned out. She explained to the porter that they wanted the seats on the platform side so she could hold Rachel up to the window to wave to Reuven.

There was a great creaking and whoosh of steam as the train pulled to a halt. Basia began issuing orders like a field commander. Miri, the oldest, held the baby. Yossel was instructed to hold on to Miri's cloak and not to let go. Basia picked up Rachel. The porter went first with their bags and secured the seats. When he came back down again, he began helping them up the steps. He took Rachel in his arms momentarily while Basia mounted and then handed her to Basia. Rachel started to lift her hand for bye-bye, but it dropped softly onto Basia's shoulder. Quickly they were inside and Basia was holding Rachel up to the window. Basia picked up Rachel's hand and began waving it for her.

Reuven stood on the platform waving, waving like crazy. He could not make himself smile. He tried, but each time his lips pressed together into a grimace. It seemed to Reuven there was nothing left in the world other than this train window, himself, and the confused little face behind the glass.

It was suddenly dawning on Rachel that this was no game.

She had grown stiff in Basia's arms, stiff with rage as her hand was waved. Then her entire body began to twist and struggle. Reuven could hear her piercing furious shrieks through the glass. Rachel tried to kick the window with her feet, but Miri came to her mother's side and held them tightly. Rachel leaned toward the window, having freed one little fist, and began to pound on the glass. Her face was glazed with tears. Reuven watched, transfixed by the enormity of her fury.

And the words of Lovotz came back so clearly in his ear. It was as if Lovotz were standing beside him on that platform. *"If I am not for myself, who will be for me? But if I am only for myself, what am I? And if not now, when?"*

Part II

RUSSIA

1900

FIFTEEN

"LIEUTENANT VACHEK, first munitions officer, reporting." Reuven Bloom snapped a smart salute to the officer of the day.

"Your papers?" the officer replied.

Reuven drew out his forged orders from the inside pocket of his uniform. He was always nervous when he presented the papers but especially now. It was the first time he had used papers done by the new forger in Moscow. Of course, half of these soldiers couldn't read anyhow—at least the ones in these units. Hardly the elite, mostly made up of ragtag hooligans who only lived for their ration of three fingers of vodka a day, as promised by the tsar. Still, Reuven never got over the fear. When one did, when one became too confident, he was killed, like Jacob Pinsk.

Jacob had been their best demolition man—their best wracker—but then something happened. He got cocky. He started taking outrageous risks. He not only blew himself up, but he also exposed the whole scheme the demolition team had used. It took them months to invent a new system, train people, and begin to implement the attacks. So far it had worked. In some ways it was superior to the previous methods. Reuven had become the key to this new system. Because his Russian was so fluent and his hands were so nimble, they had been able to more finely target their attacks. No more blowing up innocent bystanders. Reuven had become the expert at weapons demolition. "A virtuoso!" Isaac Dorf had declared. And soon he became known as String Man, the best wracker in the demolition team. Isaac, his cousin Lovotz's friend and owner of the music shop in Vilna, had taken over as the director of the Bund in Vilna after Lovotz had been murdered.

"Virtuoso!" Reuven muttered the word in disgust. It had been months since he had had time to pick up the rather inferior violin that Isaac was able to get for him. But who would want to take a Ceruti where he often had to go? Reuven's life in the last three years had been lived in the shadows of espionage, violence, and narrow escapes. He had become one of the Bund's greatest assets, not as a labor organizer but as a spy and wracker. Reuven Bloom was known for his ability to steal anything out from under the most elite guard of the tsar's troops—everything from the finest caviar to ammunition to horses. And he had an uncanny ability to understand the mechanics of death machines—rifles, artillery, mortars, weapons of all sorts. He saw through them. He had a feel for their spring actions, the chemistry and charge of the propellants, and he possessed an almost mathematical understanding of the trajectories of the projectiles. As Reuven saw through these machines of death, they became abstract to him. He neatly analyzed them the way he had once analyzed the structure of a concerto—coolly, without passion. It was only when he played that the passion had come. But as a wracker, the passion never came, which was the way it should be. For just as he had so coolly analyzed, so had he rationalized: he was not really killing. He was just blowing up the killing machines. If a rifle exploded in a soldier's face, so be it. There was one less rifle and one less soldier to kill innocent people.

Never had his talents been more valued than in the past eighteen months. Alarmed by the strikes in Minsk two years before, the tsar had stepped up his efforts against all revolutionary activities. Close to five thousand people had been arrested within the last year and a half. Most of them were Jews, but many were not. Two thousand had been exiled to Siberia, and the unrelenting pogroms continued with a growing ferocity and destruction because of improved weapons. It was said that the tsar and tsarina had stopped spending money on their favorite jeweler, Fabergé, who made the fantastic porcelain eggs inlaid with jewels, and instead were spending it on guns like the new ones into which Reuven had become so skillful at slipping thermite.

He now set to work on the shells for the artillery guns. He had announced to the ordnance officer that he wanted the shells stacked by the emplacements, and he had brought along devices for measuring and weighing them.

"Many irregular shells have been issued from one factory near Kiev and we must be assured these are not among your supply. They can be very dangerous," Reuven had said. That was his cover story. What he intended to do was to make the existing shells useless. If he removed the detonators in the middle of the shells and replaced them with duds, the artillery missiles would launch shells that never exploded. He worked quickly. He had managed to compartmentalize his mind in situations like this. His concentration was fully on unlocking the detonators and inserting the duds. Yet another part of his mind was alert to the approach of any soldier. He always explained that what he was doing he must do by himself, as it was dangerous. Accidents could happen, and he must not be distracted by idle chatter.

He had worked this ploy twice now over a period of several months, at encampments widely spread apart so that no pattern could be detected. But he and his immediate superior at the Bund knew that this would be the last time. Such ploys had a limited lifetime, especially when they depended on impersonation and were basically done in broad daylight. There were other ploys, however, that could be played time and time again. They were more dangerous too.

Reuven felt someone approaching now. "Get back!" he yelled without turning around. "Didn't the commanding officer tell you this is dangerous work, checking these shells?"

"Sorry, sir. I was just asked to request that you look at the newest shipment of regimental rifles."

What luck! Reuven thought. *Let me at those rifles.* Too bad he had not brought more bits of thermite with him. One small little slug of thermite could destroy the entire barrel of a rifle. Once a cartridge was fired, the thermite chip began to heat up to such a ferociously high temperature that the insides melted down.

When Reuven had finished with the artillery, he

was led to a shed where there was a table stacked with the new regimental rifles. Reuven opened his eyes wide. He had heard about these new guns. They were the smokeless-powder rifles. They fired jacketed lead bullets, and used not the ordinary black powder, but powder made from something called gun cotton, which was much more powerful and burned more efficiently. The bullets weighed a half ounce or less and could travel at a velocity of over six hundred meters a second. They were the deadliest of rifles. But with a chip of thermite, they would be useless forever.

When Reuven had finished his work, he was invited in to have a drink with the commanding officer. He refused, as he always did. He never liked to give anyone too much time to study his face or listen to his voice. Although he knew his Russian was perfect, he still feared that perhaps some slight tinge of a Yiddish accent might creep in, especially if he were drinking vodka. So he declined the invitation and went on his way.

His horse, which had been stolen for him a few days before, carried him in the direction of Nikolayev. He had his orders. He was to stop at a farm on the outskirts of Nikolayev. At the farm were sympathizers, non-Jews but very helpful, and he would leave his horse with them as payment for all they had done to assist the various Bund agents. He would also leave his uniform with them. They would keep it in case he needed it again, although everyone had pretty much agreed that this strategy had been exhausted. He was then to proceed into the city where at seven in the evening he would go to the café across from Alexandra Park. At the café he was to sit in the far northwest corner. Another agent would meet him. He would come to his table and say, "Do you still take your tea black as fish eggs?" It was this agent who would tell him of his next assignment.

Reuven found the farmhouse and the farmer. They offered him a plate of pickled herring and a glass of tea. The wife gave him a big lump of sugar. He knew it was expensive. "Thank you," he said quietly. He placed the lump of sugar in his mouth and sipped the tea so it strained through it. A shaft of sunlight fell across the wooden table. There was a vase of flowers, field flowers, delicate and pale in color. Reuven was savoring this moment. There were so few in his life like this—quiet, domestic, a lump of sweetness in his mouth, a slant of sunshine through the window. A little face peeked around the kitchen door.

"Aaah!" he said softly. It was a little girl, about the age that Rachel had been when she left for America what seemed like ages ago.

"Won't you come out and visit me?" Reuven asked in a gentle voice. She peeked out again, a little farther this time.

"Come, Katrina. Come say hello to the nice fellow," said the farmer.

"I have a sister. She was just your age when I last saw her. She lives in America now," Reuven said.

The little girl finally stepped into the kitchen. The mother put a bun on a plate for her. She shyly walked over to the table and climbed up onto the stool. Reuven turned to the mother.

"May I show her a trick with these spoons?" he asked.

"Of course," said the woman.

Reuven took two spoons and balanced the handle of one in the bowl of the other. With a quick, sharp tap of his fingers, he struck the handle of the first spoon. The second spoon flipped up in the air. The little girl was delighted.

"Again!" she cried.

He did it again and again and again. *How good this life could be*, he thought. How much he missed Rachel. Would he be able to hold out long enough for the revolution? Would he survive? Would he ever devote endless hours to practicing a Brahms concerto? Would he ever play games with his little sister again?

SIXTEEN

REUVEN FOUND the café easily enough. It afforded him a good view of Alexandra Park, which was lovely and green. He saw children rolling hoops along the pathways. Others rode on bicycles. There was a balloon vendor and a man with a cart selling pastries and tea by the glass. He saw several parents leading children who clutched toy boats, so he assumed there was a pond somewhere in the park where these boats could be sailed. How in the world did these two realities that were Russia exist? How could there be such a lovely park where sweets were sold and children played with toy boats within fifteen kilometers of a town that had just been burned and all the inhabitants murdered by the troops of the tsar for whose wife this park was named? What kind of God allowed this to go on?

Sometimes Reuven wondered if things were not only not improving, but possibly getting worse. Since he had joined the Bund in Vilna, there had been more than three hundred strikes, and yet more Jews were imprisoned now and more Jews had been sent to Siberia than ever before. Was it worth it? Had it been worth it? Worth what? He had sent his dear Rachel to America. He had given up his dreams of being a concert violinist. The high holy days of Yom Kippur and Rosh Hashanah were coming, but how long had it been since he had celebrated them? Or a seder? He could not even bear to think of Hannukah.

Reuven reached into his pocket and drew out his pouch of tobacco and cigarette wrappers. Smoking was a nasty habit he had picked up in the last couple of years. He looked at his fingers. They were brownish yellow with stains from the tobacco. They were the same fingers that still on occasion played the violin. No violinist's calluses anymore. His fingering technique, Herschel had said, was slightly odd—"But it works! It works." Herschel was gone. So was his father, Reb Itchel. Murdered like his parents and Shriprinka. He had never met anyone who had ever heard of a survivor from Berischeva except for himself and Rachel.

The waiter came, and the tea was very black. It was not a minute after the waiter set down the tea that Reuven sensed that the man who had just entered the café was the one he had been expecting. The agent. He was fairly tall, with pale reddish hair and a very full beard.

"Do you still take your tea black as fish eggs?" The voice was rough and grainy.

Reuven looked up. His breath caught in his throat. He knew this face. He would know this face anywhere. The man peered back, astounded. "Reuven?"

"Muttle?"

"Oh my God! You're alive. I heard everyone was killed." Muttle grabbed both Reuven's arms as if to assure himself that the man who stood before him was real. He patted his shoulders then squeezed them hard.

"I'm alive . . . that's nothing. How about you? You're not . . ." But he stopped himself before he could say "You're not in the tsar's army anymore?"

Muttle seemed to recover his wits faster than Reuven. "Follow me. We can't really talk here. We are just two old friends meeting." He reached over and hugged Reuven and whispered in his ear. "Good friends remeeting after years. The best cover of all."

Reuven paid the bill, and the two walked off arm in arm. *The man has become a bear*, Reuven thought. Muttle was a head taller than himself and had immense shoulders. They walked down an alley and then turned into a building. They went up a narrow flight of rickety stairs.

Muttle opened the door. "No key. No lock. Nothing to steal but ideas."

"No books, Muttle? I can't believe it. No Talmud?

How can you survive? You breathed words, Muttle."

"I've still got the words up here." Muttle tapped his head. "You've still got the music." He softly touched Reuven's ears.

"I hope so." Reuven smiled weakly.

"Of course you do!" Muttle gave him a hearty punch on the shoulder. "Let me see your fingers."

"No calluses," Reuven said almost sheepishly as he held out his hands.

"Ah, when the revolution comes, you'll have plenty of time for those kinds of calluses, my friend!"

The physical transformation of Muttle was almost too much to take in. How had this hairy bearish man grown out of that frail pallid boy?

"I don't know how long you were in the tsar's army, but something must have agreed with you, Muttle. You are huge."

"Believe me, it wasn't that it agreed with me at all. Quite the opposite. It disagreed. Every day they would beat me up. There was one nice old ordnance officer. I don't know why but he took a liking to me. He had been a boxer and he made me his cause. He taught me how to fight. That is something you don't find in *cheder*—a fellow who teaches you how to fight. Argue yes, but not box. So this fellow Vassily, he teaches me, first defensive. Then he starts beefing me up for offensive. He sneaks me extra rations. He makes me run and sweat and lift weights. In two weeks I learn the strategies. In six months' time, I can defend myself. These fellows, they don't think at all. They rely completely on muscle. So what I lack in muscle, I more than make up for in strategy. It is not totally different from arguing Talmud—you look for back-door entries, you learn how to lead your opponent into a corner not of faulty logic but of misplaced punches that wear him out."

So, thought Reuven, *he too must analyze and then rationalize. That is what is required to become a revolutionary.*

"But then what happened?" he asked.

"I learned all I could from Vassily. I wasn't getting beaten up anymore. I begin to think, Hell I am a fighter. Why should I let the tsar have such a champ as myself? So I joined the Bund." He paused. "But I am not like you, String Man."

Reuven chuckled. "So you heard."

"Of course I heard, but I didn't know why they called you that. I just know they say you are one of the best wrackers. I thought maybe the nickname had to do with your wire-laying abilities, the dynamiting of that munitions factory near Minsk. I had no idea it had to do with violins. I thought it was for the fuses—that the string in 'String Man' referred to the fuses." He chuckled to himself and shook his head.

"Oh yes, that too. But in Vilna where I joined the Bund, before I started working with the explosives and wracking, I sometimes played in a chamber music group—we all became wrackers, as it turned out. I took the name String Man. There was flute man, an oboist—now known as Oblow!"

"Oblow! Yes. I've heard of him."

"Yehudi Binder, a wonderful oboe player. He's working in the north now."

"So do you miss it?" Muttle asked him suddenly.

"Miss what?"

"The playing."

"I play sometimes."

"You know what I mean, Reuven. The studying, the complete immersion, your head full of concertos, notes spilling out of your ears."

Reuven laughed softly and stuck a finger in his ear to scratch it. "I do try to protect my ears working so much with explosives. Of course I am never that close, if I am lucky. If I do my job right, I am miles away by the time the artillery guns blow up or jam. Tell me. Do you miss the studying?"

"No! Not at all. It was, I realize now, an indulgence."

"An indulgence?"

"What is the point of arguing with old rabbis about what God means when what we need to be doing is making a revolution? Arguing about God's meaning when millions of people are starving, oppressed, can't make a decent wage? No, I don't need God or any books explaining him. And I take it you don't either, String Man. I heard about what the String Man did over near Smorgon when the troops came in to gun down those strikers."

Reuven looked off into space, not meeting Muttle's gaze. *Revolution*, Reuven thought. He was almost sick of the word. It didn't seem like revolution to him. Their world had not been turned upside down. It just seemed broken. He felt as if he were standing knee-deep in the shards of wrecked lives, wrecked ideas, wrecked love. There was a dissonance, an all-encompassing dissonance, the shrillness of which was almost unbearable. He felt that if he didn't get out, his eardrums might shatter.

"Hey, Reuven, what about Smorgon? Tell me about it," Muttle pressed.

"Yeah, that was quite something."

"Quite something—an entire regiment's rifles jam at the same moment when they had all these strikers lined up against a wall for a firing squad execution? My God! How did you do it?"

"Easy. I got in the night before. Replaced their supply of percussion caps with ones filled with sand from the Black Sea, and a little thermite."

"Astounding." *It wasn't at all astounding*, Reuven thought. It was simple. Half the regiment had been drunk the night before. He had been prepared. He merely went in and swapped the caps. How vulgar this conversation suddenly seemed to him.

"So you really don't miss it all?" Reuven asked Muttle again.

"I told you, I've got it all up here." He tapped his head again. "And as I said, it is an indulgence. What is a world of words without a world of action? It cannot all be endless talking, talking, talking, picking at text." He paused and his mouth curled into an almost bashful smile. "Sometimes you just have to blow something up. It was astounding what you did at Smorgon—and to think I didn't even know it was you. My best friend from Berischeva. Oh, Reuven what justification. You redeemed all those who died there."

Reuven wanted to say no. He wanted to scream no. How could Muttle be saying this? The air in the little room had suddenly grown hot and fetid. It smelled almost like the study house, full of unwashed old rebbes sweating in their gabardines, belching their sauerkraut and herring odors. How could Muttle be saying these things now, Muttle who in his scholarly days cut into words and their meanings with all the skills and precision of a surgeon with a scalpel?

But he *was* saying these things. "Smorgon was the most fantastic piece of work ever. So many of us wished we could have been there to see those rifles jam—the look of disbelief . . . it was a work of art."

It was destruction, thought Reuven. A lot of the rifles not only jammed but also blew up in the soldiers' faces. How could Muttle be discussing this now as a work of art? As redemptive? Reuven never for one minute regretted what he had done at Smorgon, but it was what it was—a violent attack on men who were murderers themselves. It was not redemptive and it was not a work of art. Is this what happened to revolutionaries? Did they lose their sense of artistic and human values? Was everything reduced to what constituted survival of one group and destruction of another? Was this the motivating moral precept by which all things must be judged and measured? But if all the oppressed people were saved, what then?

Would they know how to listen to a Brahms concerto? Would a piece of music move them so deeply that tears would fill their eyes? Would words—words of the Talmud, words of Shakespeare—stir their hearts? He looked at Muttle standing there, so different now from what he had been. He searched for the pale, fragile boy who had quivered like a leaf in the wind. *"You'll be like a living book, Muttle."* Wasn't that what Reuven said to him all those years back? *"You'll have the memory, the tradition for everyone right up here."* But now he wasn't so sure. He probably did have the words up there where he had tapped his head, but what if he could not attach them to any meaning? What if meaning had vanished?

And he remembered how Muttle had said years before that the world did not need two living books, for who would be left to play the music? *"You carry the music, Reuven. I carry the words."* But had the music receded too? Could Reuven string the notes into phrases to create melody to reveal tone to make meaning? He wasn't so sure.

Reuven looked at his friend and tried to piece together fragments of the Muttle he had known. Muttle was now jabbering on about the Bund, about the girls—"Aaah, lovely girls, and so uninhibited. I think the best thing about the revolution is the liberation of the women. It is ultimately the liberation of the men. Marriage is bourgeois."

But do you feel anything at all? Or is love only a revolutionary act? Reuven wondered. But he did not ask. Instead he got to the business at hand. "So, Muttle, speaking to me as an agent, for that is why we were to meet, I take it that you were supposed to give me my next assignment."

"Yes, yes of course." Muttle busied himself with his pipe. He seemed to sense that there would be no more shared intimacies, that the meeting was shifting to a firm business footing.

"Well, the game is up with the String Man in the Cossack uniform of the elite guard. Now we feel that you should begin growing a beard. We are temporarily going to use your talents in a somewhat new way. Not so much as a wracker, but as a deliverer."

"Deliverer of what?" Reuven liked the sound of the word.

"No explosives here. You shall be delivering people."

"People?"

"Often families. Things are worse than ever in the Pale. Especially around here—Nikolayev, Kiev. It's a hot spot for the secret police. Every day scores of Jews are being arrested for nothing, absolutely nothing. God knows where they are sent. And they arrest the women too, with increasing frequency. Now there is a new minister, Von Plehve. He's been around for a while, but everyone says he will soon be made head of the secret police. He is a master of propaganda. That massacre in Buvok was his doing. There wasn't a Cossack in sight; he let the Ukrainian peasantry do the dirty work. He started a rumor, he and his henchmen, about a ritual killing done by Jews for Passover—the murder of a Christian child whose blood was drunk as one of the four cups of wine at the seder table." Reuven had heard about this. It was a horrid, grisly story.

"So that was Von Plehve's doing?"

"Yes. We can't wait for him to strike again. We actually have an assassination team training as we speak, but the fellow is slippery. In the meantime, we are helping families escape. It's not easy. They have to go out under all sorts of covers. Some recently left dressed up as Russian Orthodox priests, if you can believe that. If we can get enough Cossack uniforms, the men can go as soldiers. We have stuffed children and small women into barrels with air holes drilled and put them out as supply convoys. In any case, we get them out of town, some way. There is a strange fellow we use to do a lot of the driving. His name is Wolf. He works in a factory on the edge of the city. Wolf drives them under cover to a few miles south of Chev. You know Chev?"

Reuven nodded.

"And that is where you meet them with a wagon and supplies. They are usually tired and hungry. But there is a forest there where they can hole up to recover. I'll show you the exact spot on the map."

"And where do I get the wagon?"

"Anywhere you can."

"And I don't go with them from there?"

"No. They must make it on their own. But between there and the border it has been very quiet the last few months. They must get as far as Nimsk the first night, and then within another day they are at the Bug River and the border."

"My work sounds easy enough."

"Compared to what you've been doing, it's easy." Muttle paused and lifted a finger. "And oh, by the way, if you can get your hands on a pot of chicken soup for when you meet them, it really helps. Put it in a jug and wrap it in blankets. They are always terribly cold by the time they get to the forest outside of Chev."

"So when do I go?"

"Well, that's the hard part. You have to have patience. We are never sure when a family or whoever is going to pass through. We have to rely quite a bit on Wolf and when he can help them. And this Wolf is a peculiar fellow. He came from Vishnagova—you know of it?"

Reuven did know. Vishnagova, a much larger town than Berischeva, had been destroyed in one of the worst pogroms in history. He had not known of anyone who had survived. But then again, no one had known that he and Rachel had survived Berischeva. Maybe if you survived when everyone else had died, it made you strange. Maybe he appeared strange to Muttle.

"We shall get a message to you when the time comes. In the meantime, it is good for you to go to that café every day, around the same time we met there this evening. For that is where an agent will find you."

Then Muttle resumed the business of packing and lighting his pipe. Perhaps pipes were good, for they helped people over the awkward bits in conversation. One did not have to look at the other person; one could become totally absorbed in this mindless, rather messy activity.

"And, Reuv, it is not good that we hang around together too much—you know, for security. The place, as I said, is swarming with secret agents."

"Yes, yes, of course."

"But there will be time again for us." Muttle still did

not look up from his pipe. A small rain of tobacco bits fell onto his shirtfront. He struck a match and puffed madly. Something began to glow in the pipe's bowl. He removed the stem from his mouth and expelled a large puff of smoke. "Yes in the future, after the revolution—comrades!" His light brown eyes looked through the swirls of smoke.

"Comrades," Reuven said weakly. Then he turned to leave.

He found the place on Kliminsky Street where it had been arranged for him to stay. It was a dingy little basement room with one narrow soot-stained window that let in a weak sliver of light. It was damp. There was a coal-burning stove, but the ventilation was so poor he was sure that he would asphyxiate himself. He stretched out on the dirty mattress. In a corner across the room he had his small bundle of belongings, even smaller now that he did not have the Cossack uniform. Heavy serge trousers, boiled wool shirts, some underwear, his violin, and yes, a small volume of Shakespeare. That was it. He did not feel hungry, nor did he feel like a drink. He felt as if he were in some strange state of suspension.

He did not quite believe what had just happened. It had an aura of unreality about it. If he were asked to describe his reunion with his long-beloved and lost friend Muttle, the word that would first pop into mind was "trick." But perhaps he too had appeared as some sort of trick to Muttle. He had changed as well. There was no denying it. He was no longer the violin prodigy. He was String Man, explosives virtuoso. Still, it did not make it any easier. This man who called himself Muttle was not the Muttle Reuven had mourned and yearned for.

He remembered so vividly those first days that stretched into months after Muttle had been snatched. The pain had been terrible, the loss seemed to permeate every atom of his being, every second of every hour of his day. It was all he had thought about. In some ways it was worse than when his parents and sister were killed. Then he had had so much to think about. It was as if he didn't have time to grieve. When had there been time to mourn? But for Muttle, he had mourned. Oh, he had mourned!

Reuven walked over to the corner and opened the violin case. He tucked the violin under his chin. He raised his bow. He did not know until he set the bow to the strings what he would play. A decisive strong chord sounded. He was playing *Chaconne* by J. S. Bach, complicated and filled with harmonic beauty. He had not tried it in years. Why now? He did not know, but he was determined to play it as it should be played—decisive, the chords given great breath, sustained so as to obtain a big tone. He could hear Herschel's voice. "This is not for sissies—you play this big. . . . The up bow . . . the up bow, that is what draws out the chords. No frills, no frills, boy. This is austere. Nothing brutal, no crassness with these chords. . . . That is it, my boy . . . concentrate . . . not too abruptly on the detached notes. That is it . . ."

Reuven could almost feel the sun coming through the window of Herschel's cottage, Reb Itchel bent over his books, the wisps of his beard. Were they blending with the smoke from Muttle's pipe? *Concentrate boy . . .*

concentrate . . . He focused on the dust motes in the sliver of light circulating to his rhythm the way he had watched Reb Itchel's beard. "Now draw back and play the next measures with tenderness . . . think of the down of the baby chick . . . think of a flower trembling in a field, a butterfly flitting like gold. Shade the music . . . give it color, nothing in life is simply one color . . . shade it . . . a little dark here and a little light there. Never high noon. It is because of shadows we find light. . . ."

Reuven did not know how long he had been playing—a quarter of an hour, an hour? Suddenly he heard a timid knock on his door. He jumped up and went to open it.

"I am sorry." A woman of middle years stood before him. She wore the traditional Jewish wig of a married woman. "I do not mean to disturb you."

"Oh, no. Do I play too loud?"

"Not loud enough." She smiled shyly.

"Oh," Reuven said softly.

"I have a special request."

"Yes."

The woman started to raise her hands to her mouth as if to stop the words from coming out. She flushed.

"Go on."

"My father. He is a very old man, and before we came to the Pale, he was a music teacher at the conservatory in St. Petersburg, a pianist. He was an accompanist for the Imperial Ballet, and that is how he met my mother."

"Oh! How wonderful."

"Yes, but now he is very sick. He is in constant pain.

However, when he heard your music . . ." Another pause. "And I was just wondering . . ."

"But of course! But of course!" Reuven was jubilant. "It would be my honor to play for your father." A part of his life had started to come back to him. Reuven turned to shut his door as he followed her out. He looked back at the room. It was still the same old dingy room, but in some ineffable way it had been transformed. It was as if the ghosts of music—Herschel, J. S. Bach, even Reb Itchel, Isaac, the baron, the Cerutis—had gathered there, leaving their shadows behind, mingling with dust motes caught in the sliver of light.

SEVENTEEN

EVERY EVENING at seven Reuven went to the café, and every afternoon at three he went upstairs to the Cahans' apartment to play for Anna Cahan's father, Moses, and his wife, Sarah. He loved playing for the old man. When he arrived, Moses would be collapsed in his bed, often groaning with the pain from his illness. His face was a deathly gray color, his eyes were unfocused and sometimes rolled back in his head. But then Reuven would begin to play, and as the music swelled in the room, it was as if breath and blood were pumped back into the raglike heap in the bed. Moses' eyes would focus, his fingers would tap the rhythm on the bedsheets. Sarah would begin to smile as she saw the pain seeming to vanish from her husband's body. Anna and her husband, David, would beam happily.

Reuven often thought to himself, *I am a blessed man, for no musician has ever had such an audience.* And he played everything: Dvořák: Bach, Beethoven, Kreutzer, Paganini, Chopin, Mendelssohn, Schubert, Mozart. It didn't matter if they were violin solos or not. He would work his way around the parts for accompanying instruments. He didn't have to think about artillery and cartridges, or black powder and thermite and velocities of bullets and trajectories. He was no longer String Man the wracker. He was String Man the violinist.

So his days fell into a pleasant rhythm. He found himself thinking more and more about Rachel. She would be five now. He wrote letters to her in care of Basia. Perhaps twice a year he received letters from Basia when he went back to Vilna. Isaac saved them for him. In the last letter there was a little drawing Rachel had made. They lived on the Lower East Side of New York. Basia wrote that she had been in correspondence with his uncle Chizor who, after spending some time in San Francisco, had gone to Minnesota, where he had opened up a haberdashery shop. He was encouraging Basia and the children to come there.

"It seems cold and far," she had written.

Now as Reuven sat at his usual table in the café, he tried to remember that map of America he had looked at nearly five years ago. He had been fifteen; now he was almost twenty. He had grown a thick mustache. Not a beard, the beard interfered with the violin.

He had just ordered another glass of tea when the rowdy hoots and guffaws of some soldiers coming through the door interrupted his pleasant daydreams. *They are such boors, all of them.* That was his last conscious thought before his blood ran cold. The soldiers took a table next to him.

"Play us a tune, Fyodor!" said one of the soldiers.

The man drew something from a case. A warm light emanated from the violin case like a small sun rising in the smoke of the café. Reuven's eyes locked onto the violin. *His* violin! His Ceruti from Berischeva, stolen on that bloody night. He held tightly on to his glass of tea. This simply could not be. Carefully he lifted his eyes toward the man. The pasty pockmarked face. The large pit in the side of his nose. The dark red eyebrows. The pieces began to reassemble themselves. It was a bland face, exceedingly bland, but it was the face of a killer.

The man lifted the violin and tucked it under his chin. His large meaty fist encircled the bow. A thin wail came out of the violin and then a cheap little staccato tune. It was all Reuven could do not to rip the instrument from the soldier's hands.

"He plays good," one of the soldiers said as he turned to Reuven and smiled quickly.

"Yyyess," Reuven stammered. In a split second he was back to his senses. He nearly thanked the soldier who had turned to him, for he had been on the brink of standing up and taking the violin. But now he would do nothing like that. He would be patient. He would watch this man, he would follow him, and when they were alone, he would kill him. His task was clear. His focus absolute. Nothing else mattered.

So began the strangest interlude in Reuven Bloom's life. If anyone asked how long he had stalked the Cossack who had murdered his sister, he would not have been able to say exactly. A few days, no, more like a week, possibly two weeks, maybe the better part of the month. He would learn so completely this Cossack, his habits, his gestures, his small idiosyncrasies, as perhaps only a mother knows a young child. Reuven began following him that night, always at a careful distance. The soldiers left the café and went to another for dancing.

Unfortunately the man never left the violin unattended. But even if he had, Reuven was not sure he would have stolen it back right then. His object was to kill; reclaiming his violin was secondary. One night, the man danced with several coarse young women. He steered them about the floor in a rough manner with those hands, the same hands that had pumped a bullet into Reuven's sister's chest. After the dancing café, the man went to another place. It was a smoky den filled with Russian soldiers. By midnight they were very drunk and had decided to go into Alexandra Park. Throwing stones at the swans in the pond was their sport. They were too drunk to hit anything. Finally at two in the morning, they began to head across town. There were some gray stone buildings, barracks, on St.

Peter Street. The guard opened the gates and the drunken soldiers tumbled into the courtyard, half carrying one another. The soldier named Fyodor, his sister's murderer, still clutched the violin case.

Reuven would not return home to his basement room that night. He slept in some bushes across the street from the barracks. At dawn he was up. Completely alert, untired, charged with energy. He had already checked the other gates that entered the courtyard. This was the main one. He was pretty sure that the others were not often used. But he climbed a tree, and from this perch he could see into the courtyard, observing the barracks and the movement of people within. If soldiers began moving toward another gate, he would be able to tell.

He did not have to wait long for Fyodor. He came out of the gate shortly after six o'clock in the morning with another soldier, an officer of higher rank. Damn! Was this fellow never unaccompanied? He and the officer headed down the street to the ordnance buildings and entered. Reuven waited. In an hour, Fyodor emerged with another man, not a soldier. *Aah!* thought Reuven. *Fyodor must be an ordnance inspector or purchasing officer.* This man he was with looked like a manufacturer's representative. He would probably go with Fyodor to the factory or the warehouses. Reuven was right.

He followed the two men to a nearby mattress factory. From there Fyodor continued to a cooperage, where barrels were being made. He was alone between the two locations but he was walking down busy streets in broad daylight. *Patience!* Reuven told himself a thousand times every hour—patience. That evening, they were back in the same café.

Days slipped into evenings, evenings into mornings. He rarely left his quarry. He would win. He knew it. He would see this man's blood. He had bought himself a knife. He carried a pistol, but he wanted to plunge a knife into this man. He wanted to feel the flesh tear. So far he had been lucky that no agent had come to him with an assignment. If one came, he would have to refuse it. Killing Fyodor was now Reuven's sole purpose in life.

He had come back briefly to his basement room one morning on perhaps the seventh or eighth day that he had been following the Cossack when there was a sharp knock on the door. It was Anna. Her face was absolutely distraught. *Had Moses died?* he wondered.

"Reuven, thank God!"

"Thank God what?"

"We thought something terrible had happened to you!"

"Why?" Suddenly the awful knowledge flooded through him. He had not been to play for Moses since he had first caught sight of the Cossack.

"Oh God, Anna." Reuven muttered a curse under his breath. "I have completely forgotten . . . I . . . I . . ." he stammered. "I have had some very pressing business. However, I shall come up right now."

"That would be wonderful, but we are just so happy you are safe."

"Oh, I am safe." But an odd tone must have crept

into his voice, for he noticed that Anna seemed to stop as she was walking out the door and look at him curiously. "I shall be right up," he added.

Reuven began playing a simple Kreutzer etude. It wasn't working. He knew within the first measure. But he kept on. He could tell that Moses and Sarah were wondering as well. Anna did not seem to notice. But Moses' hand did not tap the bedsheet and his body remained rigid with its pain. It became worse. He felt as if something within him had dried up, some reservoir that held the primal materials of music had simply evaporated. His ear could not imagine the harmonics, his fingers were leaden to the vibrations of the strings, notes flew apart and left not even the dimmest tracery of their passage. He was in a strange vacuum, a vacuum he imagined that was like death itself—without air, without sound, and what was left was perhaps only the tantalizing shards of what had been music. Finally Reuven stopped.

"Perhaps today is not my day. I don't mean to make excuses, Moses, Sarah, but I prefer to come back and play when, when . . ."

Moses spoke with his eyes closed. "When you do not have other things on your mind."

The image of a gaping wound pouring with blood slashed through Reuven's mind's eye—a Cossack, his strangely pale blue eyes frozen in fear as he felt his own throat being slashed.

"Yes. Yes. Thank you for understanding."

But Reuven knew that no one except himself would understand these blood-drenched reveries that hounded him day and night.

Finally some nights later, his hour came. Fyodor and his friends were at the smoky café that was always jammed with soldiers. They normally spent an hour there. Reuven had taken up his usual perch behind some trash bins at the corner of an alley, which gave him concealment as well as a good view of the door. The soldiers had not been in the place long when he saw a figure emerge. It was Fyodor, and he was alone. Reuven could tell from the manner in which he was walking that he was not feeling well. It appeared as if he might have stomach cramps; perhaps the vodka had finally gotten to him.

"Well, let me and not the vodka finish you off," Reuven muttered. He drew the knife from a sheath inside his coat pocket. Fyodor was carrying the violin. It looked as if he was heading back to the barracks when he suddenly turned down an alley. Reuven followed in the dense shadows of the moonless night. The Cossack set down the violin and leaned against a wall. There was a retching sound.

"May I help you, my friend?" Reuven had taken a handkerchief out of his pocket.

"How kind." The eyes pale like blue ice.

"Not at all, Fyodor." The Cossack looked at him now, suddenly wary. A split second passed, and Reuven's knee jackknifed up into the man's groin. A terrible gasp, then a surge of reeking vomit poured out. He had the

Cossack on the ground. Reuven's knee pressed down on the man's chest. He gripped the knife against Fyodor's throat. How hard would he have to press it to make the first cut? To see blood? Should he slice quickly, right through the main artery to spare the man pain? One deft stroke so that he would instantly lose consciousness—the way the kosher butchers killed animals? But this man was worse than an animal. He did not deserve such sanctifying rituals. Fyodor must remain alert. Reuven stared deep into the man's eyes. He could see the delicate scrawl of blood vessels on the glazed white orbs. Fyodor was breathing, but was this really life that he now possessed? Reuven could feel his own knee rise and fall on the man's chest with his every breath. The blue eyes filled with fear, overwhelming fear. Their color seemed to become more intense, bluer. A sound came from his throat.

"Why? Why?"

"Does the animal ask why?" whispered Reuven. He was enjoying this. His head became full of engaging banter while he pressed the knife to the flesh. "Should I say a benediction before I slice your throat? That is the way of the *shochet,* the kosher butcher. What do you think of that, Mr. Fyodor? I am about to kill you according to the laws of ritual slaughter? Perhaps that is too good, eh?"

Reuven cocked his head, tipping his ear up, as if to listen for a response. There was nothing, of course. There was less than nothing. Reuven could not hear a thing. The vacuum he had experienced when playing for Moses suddenly seemed to envelop him. A cat jumped off a fence, but he did not even hear the impact as it lighted on the cobbles. A wind stirred the leaves of a tree, but Reuven heard nothing, and the sound of this man's pounding breath was swallowed into the great all-consuming silence. Had Reuven crawled into a coffin with the corpse, it could not have been more silent. The world of sound was disintegrating before him. He looked down at the knife. Fleshy folds gathered on either side of its edges. He had dreamed about this forever. He had imagined the blood. He had imagined his knee just where it was feeling the weakening pulse of the heart. Each pump draining out the blood. A metered heart, and he was here with his knee to play the beats to the end of the piece. A blood symphony.

Suddenly nothing seemed to make sense to Reuven. The blood-drenched dreams were retreating. *Stay with me, stay with me. It is all I have. All I have wanted all these years. My blood dreams. Don't leave me,* he prayed and he pressed the knife harder. But still he did not cut.

"Why?" the Cossack croaked. "Why?"

Reuven took a deep breath. A ragged voice, a voice he had never heard, came from his own throat. "I want my violin back."

There was a clatter on the cobbles as Reuven dropped the knife and then reached for the violin. He took his knee off the Cossack's chest and got up. Fyodor took a deep breath but did not move. His eyes followed Reuven.

"Good night," Reuven said, and walked away listening to his own footsteps and the beat of his heart.

EIGHTEEN

IT WAS lucky, Reuven thought, that he had managed to steal a good wagon because for the last few miles, the road had been terrible. Walking would have been preferable, but it was his understanding that this was not the walking kind of family. There were babies and an old grandfather, a mother, a father, a young woman, and a child. Reuven had managed to get a pot of chicken soup, cold by now even though he had wrapped it in layers of cloth for insulation. He had wedged it in between some sandbags that had been put in the back of the wagon for some weight. The family, he was told, would be along this pathetic excuse of a road somewhere.

He had passed a small bridge that spanned a creek. The sun was just rising, and a fierce almost blinding light spread over the horizon. He cupped his hands over his brow and squinted to see the far edge of the field. They would have spent the night at this edge near the forest, probably in the forest. Aaah! Reuven thought he saw something over there, a trace of smoke from a dying campfire. He pulled up the horse and tied it to a stump near the road. Then he took out the soup pot and some bowls and he began walking out across the field.

A middle-aged, stiff-jointed man came out from a stand of birch trees.

"Hello!" Reuven cried cheerfully to the man.

A young girl of no more than nine or ten clutched his arm and looked out from under tangles of long dark hair with enormous gray eyes.

"You are Reuven?" The man stepped forward. The little girl moved with him as if she were locked onto him.

"Reuven Bloom. Yes I am. Quick, start the fire again, I brought you soup."

Then a small distinct voice emanated from behind the tangled hair. "Do you have a firebrand?"

"What? Say that again, child?" he asked.

"Do you have a firebrand? Wolf said you were a firebrand."

For some reason Reuven thought this remarkably funny, especially coming out of a child's mouth. He hated when people laughed at children. It was so easy to hurt their feelings. But he began to chuckle, and then he could not help it. He flung back his head and laughed. When he finally recovered, he noticed that the child did not seem offended at all but was looking at him with great curiosity.

"Why don't you help me get this soup on the fire? I forgot a spoon to stir it with, however. Do you have one?"

"No." She shook her head solemnly. "But I'll find you a stick." Others began to come out of the woods. There was a woman who was introduced as Ida. She held a baby in her arms and a toddler clung to her skirts. Then there was another woman in her midtwenties who wore spectacles and a very serious expression. She reminded Reuven of the women in the cafés in Vilna. She helped an ancient-looking man who was bent over and leaning on a cane. He was introduced as Zayde Sol. He mumbled something when he was introduced, growled deeply in his throat as if to clear it of a river, and then spat on the ground.

"Charming," muttered the bespectacled woman.

"Where's Sashie?" someone asked.

"Oh Sashie, the little one—the girl, she went to fetch something to stir the soup with," Reuven replied. At that moment she came back.

"A birch stick. I peeled it myself. So it's very clean now."

"Perfect," Reuven said, and began stirring the soup with it.

The little girl called Sashie was watching him carefully. He heard her asking the woman in a low voice what a firebrand was.

"Oh, it's a revolutionary. You know what that is," the woman answered. Reuven pretended to be focused on the soup, but he was listening to the conversation.

"What do you mean, a revolutionary, Aunt Ghisa?" the little girl asked. "Is it something musical?"

Reuven nearly dropped the stick in the soup pot.

"Musical?" Ghisa said in a perplexed voice. "No. You know, it's someone who stirs things up, inflames people with ideas, tries to turn things upside down to make thing better politically."

"Huh," said the girl.

Reuven began serving up the soup first to Ida, then to Ghisa, and then to Sashie. "I did remember bowls," he said. He bent down and handed her the bowl. "Even firebrands like me still believe in serving ladies first. Here you go!" The huge gray eyes looked up and right through him. Reuven nearly flinched at the intensity of her gaze.

"You're no firebrand, Mr. Bloom. You are filled with music!"

Reuven had never felt anything like this. "Who . . . how do you know that?"

"I just know it," she said, setting down her soup bowl and folding her arms across her narrow chest.

He looked at her. There was no figuring these things out. "Just . . . just stay right there. No. I mean, get up and serve the rest of the soup while I fetch something from the wagon."

He returned a minute later with his violin. Tucking it under his chin, he put his foot on the edge of a rock. He began slowly. A procession of notes stirred the air. The sound was hushed, delicate but never frail. The girl sat on a log near his feet. He could look straight down the fingerboard and see her small fragile face. The music went right into her. He could tell. It found a resonance within her. She did not merely sense the vibrations, she became part of them. She was a completely musical creature.

Later that morning Reuven stood in the middle of the road and played his violin as the family drove off. Of all the difficult things Reuven Bloom ever had to do, this oddly enough was one of the most difficult. It was another good-bye. His entire life seemed to be made of good-byes, Reuven suddenly thought. He was very tired of it, tired of good-bye, tired indeed of revolution. The idea of leaving the Bund no longer shocked him as it once might have. Not since his meeting with Muttle. He had no more anger. He was an impatient man now and he was simply sick of standing in the wreckage of broken things.

Sashie stood up in the back of the wagon as they drove away. She stood straight and steady and never took her eyes off Reuven Bloom as he continued to play the beautiful music. The notes wrapped around her, streamed through her, and, she would later say, "filled me with stars."

Sashie stayed standing as she and Reuven grew smaller and smaller in each other's vision, until they were little specks on each other's horizons. And even when they were mere specks, the filaments of the music growing dimmer and dimmer seemed to connect them and they knew that the other was there until the wagon disappeared around a bend in the road.

NINETEEN

AMERICA, ELLIS ISLAND, NEW YORK

1904

"Bloom—B-L-O-O-M. First name, Reuven." He looked down. The man had written "Rubin" not "Reuven." Oh well. So he would be Rubin Bloom here in America. At least he had passed through all the inspection stations. Poked, prodded, and questioned by interpreters, he had been declared lice free and fit for America. The *Goldeneh Medina.* And now he was to go through the wide door and somehow among the hundreds of people on the other side, find his baby sister. But she wouldn't be a baby anymore. Rachel would be almost eight years old. The moment he stepped through the door he felt swamped, as a sea of indistinct faces, their mouths moving around the words of a dozen unintelligible languages, rushed toward him. How would he ever find Rachel? At eight she would still be too short to show up in this crowd. He scanned the faces. Would he recognize Basia? It had been six years. An adult would not change in six years as much as a child. Perhaps he should concentrate on looking for Basia.

"No smoking here! No smoking! Sir."

A voice barked, "It's not lit, you fool." Reuven turned to see what was going on. There was an odd sight, a slightly illogical assemblage in which the parts didn't quite come together. It was like sorting out the pieces of a jigsaw puzzle.

Reuven saw a burly man wearing a fashionable homburg hat with an odd contraption atop his shoulders. It loomed above his head like another hat. There was something sticking out of his mouth, and then over the wide fur lapels of his coat two skinny legs in thick wool stockings hung down. A child's arm reached over the top of the man's hat and plucked the cigar from his mouth.

"Take it out, Uncle Chizzie," she said.

"Aaach! Women!" The white tufted eyebrows flew up in exasperation.

Reuven froze. His mouth dropped open but no words came out. The other hat was no hat. The hat was a girl, no longer a baby.

"Rachel!" Reuven bellowed, and tore through the crowd, dragging his bundles. On top of her uncle's shoulders, Rachel seemed to dance. The cigar flew up and down. The homburg tumbled through the air. A cloud of white hair swirled up like a cumulous cloud.

"Chizzie!"

Then they were in each other's arms: Rachel, still on her uncle's shoulders, embracing Reuven's head; Chizzie pressing him to his chest in a bear hug. They created an amazing tangle of arms and legs.

"My God, this is your leg. Such a long leg," Reuven said, as his sister kept hugging his head. Then Rachel had scrambled down and was standing in front of him. "Such a tall girl!"

They were caught in each other's gaze. "You are so different. So big," Reuven said.

"You . . ." she paused. A slow, almost shy smile spread over her face. "You look just like Aunt Basia said you would." She gasped and flung her arms around his waist.

"So this is your old friend, the very same violin," Chizor said, and touched the wood of the Ceruti lightly. They were in Basia's apartment on Delancey Street on the Lower East Side of New York.

"How did you come to find it again?" Basia asked.

"Oh, it is too long a story for now," Reuven replied.

Perhaps too long, but also perhaps too desperate or violent. Basia and Chizor exchanged glances. There was not a refugee from Russia or Poland these days who did not harbor a terrible story.

"Besides," Reuven continued, "I want to hear your stories. How have you learned English so well, Rachel?"

"I go to school. Real school. Girls do that here in America. I sit at a desk. I write on pieces of paper. I have my own pencil box. But I know how to use a dip pen and I am learning to write cursive. We have spelling tests and geography lessons. "

"Can you tell me where the Great Lakes are?"

"That's easy. That is where Uncle Chizor lives. He came all the way from Minneapolis to be here when he heard you were coming."

"But tell Reuven how you really learned to write so well in English," Basia said.

"You mean my book, Auntie?"

"Yes, of course."

Reuven watched her as she went into the other room for her book. He had not taken his eyes off her all evening. She was indeed the very same Rachel, bigger of course and speaking English as well as Yiddish now. But her spirit was the same. He could tell. Willful, positive. It was right that he had let her come here. She now returned with a large scrapbook.

She sat down on the floor by Reuven's feet and opened it to the first page. On this page there was a lumpy-looking figure with stick legs and on his back there was a basket with a small round face peeking out. Underneath in Yiddish, written in the hand of an adult, were the words: "This is me. Rachel Bloom. On my brother's back. We leave Russia." And underneath the words was the English translation.

Miri spoke now. "We remembered when you first came to our apartment in the alley off Szeroka Street and how you told the story of carrying Rachel on your back out of Russia. It was Yossel's and my favorite story. We made Mama tell it all the time. And when Rachel learned how to talk, she remembered things and added to the story. Show him the pictures of the snow cave, Rachel." Rachel turned a few pages in the book to another drawing.

"You see," Rachel said, "I didn't know how to make snow on white paper, so I painted most of the paper blue and left the white for the cave. There are you and me, and there is the basket. There is not one picture in the book without the basket."

Reuven was mesmerized as he turned the pages of the book. The drawings became more expressive, more detailed, and the captions under the drawings grew longer. Soon there was no Yiddish, only English, written now in the wobbly hand of a child.

"So that is how you learned to write English?"

Rachel stood up and put her hand lightly on top of Reuven's. "And not to forget you."

The next morning Basia asked in a tentative voice, "So what do you think you might want to do here? There are some openings in the Katz shop."

"No!" Rachel closed a book shut and looked at her aunt. "Aunt Basia. I . . ." She hesitated and bit her lip lightly. "I don't think he should do that."

"Do what?" Basia asked.

Rachel looked down at her shoes and in a voice barely above a whisper she said, "Stitch and cut cloth."

"What should he do, then?" Miri asked.

Rachel's gaze slid toward the violin. "He must play his violin. That is what my brother does."

Rachel heard her aunt draw a deep breath.

"Perhaps you are right," Basia said carefully. "I shall make some inquiries." Rachel stole a look at her brother. He was looking at her, his eyes shiny. She bit her lip lightly and felt a flush creep up in her cheeks. It was almost as if there was a silent music between them.

Two days later Reuven was standing in the front office of the Russian Symphony Society of New York. Rachel had begged to skip school and come with them. Basia had relented. Reuven did not understand one word that his aunt was saying to the rather stern lady behind the desk. It seemed very odd to him that Rachel, on the other hand, understood every word. He watched his sister's face, for that was the best translation. She looked tense and nervous. Her eyes narrowed over something the woman behind the desk had said.

The woman wore wire-rimmed spectacles that perched on the thin ridge of her bony nose, and she was observing the three of them as a very picky bird might regard an insect, or three insects, that had crept into its path—edible or not? But apparently Basia was not ready to creep. She had stepped right up to the desk, fixed the woman with a stern gaze, and began to bark harsh words that were unintelligible to Reuven. He saw Rachel's eyes widen in amazement. Her cheeks flushed, and a smile played dangerously around the corners of her mouth.

The woman's nostrils flared and she gave a sharp rap to the papers she held in her hand so that the edges lined up. She then swiveled in her seat and turned to the typewriter and began typing. Basia moved around the corner of the desk and bent over into the woman's line of vision, then let loose with a hot string of words that Reuven did understand, for they were Yiddish. He was shocked at Basia's audacity.

Then Rachel whispered to Reuven, "She's one of those types. Aunt Basia can't stand them."

"What types?"

"An uptown German Jew. They think they're better than any of us. She's pretending not to understand Yiddish. But she does." Rachel clapped her hand over her mouth to stifle a giggle. Basia was speaking now in Yiddish.

"You understand it when I say you are a miserable little piece of pig dropping. But you want it served up with caviar? Well, you can go back and eat caviar with the *farshtinkener* tsar. That's what you can do!"

"What is this?" A rather large man with a black waxed handlebar mustache came into the room. The lady at the desk began speaking. Rachel kept interrupting. Again Reuven did not understand a word. Now he saw the lady shrug her shoulders. The man tapped Reuven on the shoulder and nodded his head, indicating that he should follow. Rachel and Basia followed as well.

They entered a small room where there was a piano. A woman was at the piano and another man was tuning a cello. There was some more talk that Reuven did not understand. Then Rachel turned to him and spoke in Yiddish.

"They want you to play. If you play well enough, they'll let you come back for an official audition. They say they don't need a violinist. But just play. Then they'll change their minds." Her dark eyes flickered brightly.

Reuven's heart raced. Standing before him was the essence of love and faith. It was almost seven years ago that he had carried her on his back out of Russia, and now she was carrying him into America.

He played part of the Dvořák *Serenade for Strings* in E major. There was a stunned silence at the end.

"More," the man with the waxed mustache said, and Reuven understood. On the night after he had let Fyodor go, on the night he found his violin and much more, he had begun to compose a piece for piano and violin that he thought of as the first of the *Miracle Suites*. Why not play it now, just the beginning, because he did not have the music with him to give to the pianist? The first notes fell clear and limpid like the first raindrops after a long drought and one could perhaps anticipate the greening to come.

Rachel was right. The New York Russian Symphony Society did not need a violinist—not one like Reuven. Ten minutes later Rachel, Reuven, Basia, and the man with the handlebar mustache were riding in a taxi uptown to Carnegie Hall. They were to meet with the conductor of the New York Philharmonic, Wassily Safonoff.

Exactly one year later Reuven Bloom made his debut as a soloist with the New York Philharmonic. In the front-row seats were his sister Rachel, his cousin Basia and her children, as well as his uncle Chizor. Just before he played the first note, with his bow raised, he listened. He listened to the creaks in the plushly upholstered seats of the house. He listened to the occasional cough from the audience. He heard the beat of his own heart. He thought of Herschel. He thought of his sister Shriprinka, his mother and father, and he thought of the music, the song begun long ago in the shtetl, broken by blood and vengeance in the horror of a single night. Now it was time to mend. Reuven Bloom drew the bow over the strings of his violin and released the notes into the air where the silence embraced them as the sky gathers birds into its blueness.

Epilogue

The immensity of Reuven Bloom's talent was immediately recognized. He toured the world. In addition to playing the violin, he became a renowned composer. One of his best-known compositions was the *Miracle Suites* for violin and piano. Ten years after arriving in America, when he was thirty-two, he met Sashie and her family once more when he gave a performance in Minnesota, where they had settled after coming to America. In the small Jewish community in Minneapolis, they had met Reuven's uncle, Chizor Bloom. Chizor arranged a reunion backstage after the concert for Sashie and her family with the man who had helped them escape from Russia nearly thirteen years before. Sashie had grown into a young woman of twenty-three. Even before Reuven met her backstage, he felt her presence in the audience. He would later say in an interview that he could never understand it, but as long as he lived, if his dear Sashie were anywhere within listening distance of his violin, he seemed to feel her listening. For him, there was a unique resonance when Sashie listened.

"It is almost," he said, "as if she is a kind of invisible fifth string for my violin."

Sashie and Reuven fell deeply in love. The same year that he married Sashie, Reuven bought a Guarneri violin for almost a hundred thousand dollars, financed by his uncle Chizor, who had found great success manufacturing men's overcoats. Reuven's sister Rachel Bloom remained in New York, where she married and became a writer. Amongst her most popular works is *The Basket Stories,* which recounts her leaving Russia on her brother's back in the grain basket.

Sashie and Reuven had three children and many grandchildren and great-grandchildren. One of those great-grandchildren was named Rachel. I am that Rachel. Some years back I wrote my Nana Sashie's story in a book called *The Night Journey*, and now it is time for me to tell Papa's story. The story of my great-grandfather, Reuven Bloom.

Historical Note

The history of Jewish persecution began long before the nineteenth century and the time of the family of Reuven Bloom. For centuries, there were almost no Jews in Russia. When Poland was partitioned among Russia, Prussia, and Austria starting in 1772, however, Russia annexed a large segment of Poland. Suddenly there was a sizable Jewish population to deal with. Beginning in 1791 during the reign of Tsarina Catherine the Great, Jews were confined to an area that came to be known as the Pale of Settlement, which was created partly to eliminate Jewish economic competition from major cities like Moscow and to guard against racial mixing. By the late 1800s, about five million Jews lived in the Pale. This constituted almost half of the Jewish population of Europe. The Pale contained twenty-five provinces that included Ukraine, Lithuania, Belorussia, Crimea, and part of Poland.

Because it was almost impossible for Jews to own farmland, small Jewish villages known as shtetls sprang up in the Pale. For the most part, the people in the shtetls spoke Yiddish, but many could also speak and understand Russian or Polish. Their life was hard. They were poor, but they still managed to have schools both religious and secular, build humble synagogues, and carry on as best they could.

For many years, Jews were forbidden to join the Russian Army. In 1827, Tsar Nicholas I reversed the law and began requiring the shtetls to fill a heavy quota of soldiers. Jewish boys were drafted at eighteen and forced to serve for twenty-five years, but were not permitted to hold the rank of officer. During their years of service they were subjected to brutal treatment and attempts at conversion.

Each shtetl usually had a ruling council that was responsible for dealing with the representatives of the imperial government. The council members usually selected which young men would go into the army. If the ruling council refused to do this task, the tsar's troops would simply come through the village and kidnap eligible boys. This same army would often storm through a Pale settlement setting fires and murdering innocent people.

In 1881, the relatively liberal Tsar Alexander II, who freed Russia's serfs and even relaxed some of the restrictions on Jews slightly, was assassinated. Many people blamed the Jews. In response to the assassination, Alexander's son—the new tsar, Alexander III—became reactionary and intolerant. By far the worst persecution of the Jews took place under Alexander III (1881–1894) and his successor, Nicholas II (1894–1917). New laws were passed in 1882 that restricted the lives of Jewish people even more. Violent anti-Semitism was officially encouraged. This only added more fuel to the anger of the Jews and the dispossessed in Russia. As conditions became increasingly bad not only for Jews but for all poor people, anger spread and the seeds of rebellion were sown. It was during the reign of Tsar Alexander III that the organized massacres known as pogroms, which had been rare, really began. More anti-Jewish laws were passed that excluded Jews from certain jobs, rights of ownership, and freedom of travel.

A great number of Jews decided to simply leave. Between 1881 and 1914, over two million Jews left Russia. Some joined a Zionist movement and went to Palestine as young settlers. Even more went to America.

Many of those who stayed behind were determined to change Russia. They became revolutionaries and sought to create a socialist nation. They formed underground groups to encourage strikes, launch protests, and sabotage the Russian army. The government usually responded with brutality.

The winter of 1904–1905 was especially harsh. People were starving, work conditions were horrendous, and the crippling war between Russia and Japan had just ended in defeat. Civil unrest was at an all-time high. The tsar and his family, however, suffered none of the indignities or the deprivations of the Russian people. Then one bitter cold January morning, 150,000 people massed in front of the Winter Palace in St. Petersburg in protest.

Russian troops fired on them, and over five hundred people were killed. This day came to be known as Bloody Sunday.

It would take twelve more years for the Russian Revolution to really begin. On March 15, 1917, Nicholas II abdicated the throne. On July 16, 1918, the tsar and his family were murdered, and on November 7 of that year, the Winter Palace was stormed and the Bolshevik Revolution began.

Rachel and Reuven are fictional creations, but their story is similar to that of the author's own grandparents. Like so many Russian Jews who had lived in the Pale, Joseph Lasky had been forced to serve in the military. A pogrom in a nearby shtetl convinced him it was time to leave. Unlike most of the Jews of that era who left for America and settled on the Lower East Side of New York City, Joseph took his family to Duluth, Minnesota, to live. The author's father, Marven Lasky, was the first child of Joseph and his wife, Ida, to be born in America.